JILLAROO

After a failed marriage, Megan travels to the Australian outback to take up a new job. She is to help run the house at Noongara Sheep Station and look after the owner's young daughter. But Megan discovers that Noongara is very different to the little farm in Wales she was brought up on. She also finds its owner, Patrick Malone, to be arrogant and temperamental. And why does he deny his lovely little daughter the love she craves? Soon, Megan finds herself caught up in the affairs of this strange household.

Neath Port Talbot Libraries Llyfrgelloedd Castell-Nedd Port Talbot

Books should be returned or renewed by the last date stamped above.

Dylid dychwelyd llyfrau neu eu hadnewyddu erbyn y dyddiad olaf a nodir uchod

NP56

DINA McCALL

JILLAROO

Complete and Unabridged

LINFORD
Leicester

First published in Great Britain in 1989

First Linford Edition
published 2005

British Library CIP Data

McCall, Dina
    Jillaroo.—Large print ed.—
    Linford romance library
    1. Ranch life—Australia—Fiction
    2. Welsh—Australia—Fiction
    3. Australia—Fiction 4. Love stories
    5. Large type books
    I. Title
    823.9′14 [F]

    ISBN 1–84395–901–1

Published by
F. A. Thorpe (Publishing)
Anstey, Leicestershire

Set by Words & Graphics Ltd.
Anstey, Leicestershire
Printed and bound in Great Britain by
T. J. International Ltd., Padstow, Cornwall

This book is printed on acid-free paper

1

The taxi dropped me at the wide entrance to Noongara Sheep Station. I stood watching it disappear in a cloud of dust and exhaust fumes. Heat came shimmering up from the baked earth to meet me, and I wished — not for the first time that day — that I had arrived looking less like a grease spot.

I lifted the latch on the long, white-painted five-bar gate, and taking a fresh grip on my suitcases, pushed my way through it and kicked it shut. Then I walked the few yards up the path that led to the house, a large sprawling wooden building, one-storeyed except for the centre section which had a long shallow roof. I trudged wearily up the steps of the long shaded verandah. I dumped the cases outside the door of the homestead. Running my fingers through hair that was clinging damply to my neck, I looked around me.

So this was it. My new home. My new job. It was a far cry from the little farm I had been brought up on, back in Wales — the other side of the globe. In spite of the strain of the journey and all that had gone before it I couldn't help but feel a thrill of excitement . . . but it was tinged with a breath of apprehension. *Would* the owner of all this consider me suitable, once he met me?

Well, I told myself with determination, there was only one sure way of finding out. For the umpteenth time that day I fished in my shoulder bag and dragged out the dog-eared envelope.

The door won't be locked, the letter, signed, 'on behalf of Patrick Malone' stated. *Walk straight in.* You couldn't be friendlier than that. My spirits rose as I put my hand on the door knob.

It was torn from my grasp, and a whirlwind stormed out to collide with me, a heavy boot crushing my sandalled toes. I squealed and would have fallen

— if the man hadn't caught me.

Blue eyes burned into mine. They blazed angrily down from a bronzed face that was all angles — angry eyes and tawny, copper hair. Like a lion! I thought incoherently, as I reeled from the impact. His arms felt like steel, clasping me tightly. I had to tilt back my head to look from my mere five foot three inches up into his face; he was a tall man, and broad-shouldered, but lean and wiry. Somehow I knew this must be my prospective employer, and it struck me that we might stay frozen for ever in this ridiculous position, if one of us didn't say something.

'Mr Malone?' I gasped. 'I'm Megan Roberts, and . . . and you can let me go now, if you don't mind.'

He abruptly released his grip, and scowled.

'Sorry. But d'you usually barge in without warning?'

'Your letter said to go straight in. If you'd mentioned you were in the habit of flying out of doors like that, I might

3

have shouted from a safe distance.' It came out all sing-song. Indignation always brought out the Welsh in me.

His eyebrows raised. '*My* letter? I've only just learned of your existence — and as far as I'm concerned you can go back to where you came from.' He gave a sour grin. 'That should be far enough.'

So I was the object of his ill humour? But it didn't make sense. What could he have against me — we had only just met? Not that I cared one way or the other, except where the job was concerned. I glared straight back into his blue eyes, antagonism sparking the air between us.

'Blue? What have you done?' A woman's voice interrupted. 'Is she all right, or have you crippled the girl? That's all we need, two of us on crutches! Bring her inside.'

Before I could identify the owner of the voice my feet were swept from under me again, and I was cradled easily in the man's arms as he carried

4

me into the cool interior of the house. I only had time to register shock at this second assault before he dumped me unceremoniously on a sofa. I blinked at the change from harsh sunlight to the shade of the room, and protested as he crouched beside me.

'There's no need. You only trod on my toe, for goodness' sake.'

He treated me as though I hadn't spoken, and drew off my sandal. His hands cupped my foot, dusty though it was from travelling, and it looked tiny in his broad palm as he twisted it this way and that.

He looked up quickly. 'Did that hurt?' His face was level with mine, those penetrating eyes looking straight at me, but there was no concern in his face . . . no interest even.

'No,' I answered sharply. 'There's nothing wrong with me.'

Nothing but a feeling of vulnerability, my bare foot wrapped in his brown hands. I didn't like the feeling. I didn't like the intimacy of it. My insides were behaving in a most peculiar fashion. Shock, no doubt — or the long and tiring journey.

'You'll live,' he said, and he sounded as if he couldn't care a jot whether I did, or not.

'No thanks to you!' broke in the woman. 'My dear . . . let me introduce myself. I'm Peg Malone . . . sister to this ungrateful creature. And he, of course, is Patrick . . . usually called 'Blue'. Because of his hair, you know.'

I did know. It was one of those odd Australian customs, that people with red hair were called 'Blue'. Not that his *was* red exactly, I thought as he still kneeled beside me — seemingly having no inclination to relinquish my foot — more the colour of burned rock, as if he had sprung ready made from the harsh landscape of the outback.

'I was the one who put in the advert,' his sister continued, 'on Blue's behalf, I might add.'

I tore my bemused gaze away from the tawny head so close to mine, and

6

focused on the woman for the first time. The resemblance was obvious. Peg Malone was an older edition of her brother. Her hair was not as fiery as his, but she had a strong pleasant face, and in spite of balancing on crutches she was holding out a hand in welcome.

'You seem to have broken the ice, if nothing else.' She grinned. 'Wish I'd been so lucky. I've been real crook since I came off my horse. Glad you've taken the job, Miss Roberts.'

I reached up over Blue's head to shake Peg's hand, warming to her. 'I'd rather you just called me Megan. And . . .' I added just to put the record straight, 'it's not Miss . . . it's Mrs.'

'She's married?' Blue rose to his feet in one fluid movement, and confronted his sister. 'You never said she was married!'

'You never asked. Anyway, I didn't know myself.'

He banged his fist on a nearby table. I jumped, watching them both in disbelief, as I struggled to refasten my sandal. Was this family always so volatile?

'She's married — but it won't have escaped you that she's here, alone. And you think she's suitable to look after the child . . . she's left her Pommie husband, no doubt, and is on the lookout for the next one. Well, she needn't look here!'

'Blue! I can't manage the house and Jinny on my own, while I'm like this. Be reasonable. I thought I was doing you a favour.'

'Don't give me that!' His eyes glittered angrily. 'You know my feelings. You'd no right to take her on without my permission. She's not needed. Melody could have helped out.'

'Melody's hired to cook and wash for the hands, not to be a nanny to your child.'

So far they had both ignored me. My blood began to boil. If there was anything I hate, it's being talked about as if I'm not there.

'May I get a word in edgeways?'

They swung around as if surprised to see that I was still with them, but I was determined to have my say.

'I'd like to point out that I did *not* leave my 'Pommie' husband, as you so rudely called him. He ran out on me. He went back to England . . . with somebody else. We were divorced a couple of months ago.'

The facts sounded balder and bleaker than ever, put like that. So few words for the end of all my dreams . . . it made me angry that I had even had to voice them, dragging out the tattered fabric of my life in front of strangers. I pulled myself up as tall as I could, and scowled up at Blue. 'Not that it's any business of *yours.*'

'Isn't it?' He stared down at me. What was he — six foot three, or four maybe? He seemed a giant. There was a twitch to his lips I could not fathom. 'I'd say it was very much my business, since it's my home you want to live in.'

'Well you needn't worry.' My dander was up now, and it seemed I had nothing to lose. I could be just as rude as he was. He deserved it. 'I've no intention of polluting your home one moment longer than I need to. I'll take the next coach back to Perth, and then make my way back to Sydney, but before I go I'd like to say you are — without doubt — the rudest man I've ever had the misfortune to meet.'

He stared, and I held my breath. Had I prodded the lion too hard? I had the absurd impression he was about to spring, but to my relief he just shrugged. The anger died in his eyes, to be replaced by a bleak, shuttered look. Then he turned towards the door.

'Suit yourself.'

Before I could say another word he slammed out of the house.

'That's tellin' him!' Peg said with relish. 'But it's a shame, all the same. I'm sure you'd have suited just fine.'

What had I done! I'd crossed a continent on the strength of this job. If I left now, what would I do? Where would I go? I had very little money left.

This was to have been the end of the line for me — the place where the running had to stop, and a new life begin.

With a stammered word of apology to Peg, I flew out of the door after him, past my abandoned suitcases, and down the steps.

'Mr Malone. Please . . . please wait.'

He had already disappeared past the row of tall, stringy-bark gums that separated the house from the yard and outbuildings, but I raced across the yard and caught up with him as he reached the largest of the sheds. He wheeled around to face me, and the look on his face made me falter.

'Look . . . I'm sorry,' I blurted. 'I shouldn't have spoken like that. Obviously there's been some sort of mix-up. I was told there was a job, helping to run the house . . . and that you needed someone to look after your daughter. I thought you knew I'd applied for the job.'

He didn't speak, just stood with

exaggerated patience, waiting for me to finish. I'd never before met a man who made me feel so awkward . . . so self conscious. Those piercingly blue eyes looking at me so steadily, unnerved me — but since he still didn't speak, I plucked up the courage to carry on.

'After all, it's not *my* fault your sister hired me without telling you, and I *have* come a long way at considerable expense. I'm not afraid of hard work . . . and . . . and I like children.'

I waited for him to say something — anything — but he stood impassively, slowly looking me over, giving no hint of what he was thinking. I moved uneasily, intensely conscious of my travel-stained appearance. My sleeveless cotton dress clung to me. I could feel the sun burning through it.

'Mr Malone,' I said softly, desperation forcing a note of pleading into my voice. 'Obviously your sister *does* need help. And . . . frankly, I need this job.' I swallowed. Humbling myself went against the grain . . . and *particularly* to this man. 'Since you seem to dislike me,' I went on nervously, 'I could keep out of your way. I wouldn't be any trouble . . . '

He moved then, unexpectedly. For a big man it was surprising how quick and lithe his movements were. He put his hands on my shoulders, and I was pinned against the shed wall, unable to move. As he bent his head to stare into my startled face, I faltered into silence. I could feel a flush rising, its heat travelling in a wave up my neck and into my cheeks. Scanning my face, as though searching for something, he swore quietly.

'Girl . . . you stand there, looking like that . . . and you say you'll be no trouble.' He gave a short, cynical laugh. Then he straightened up. 'OK. I'm probably off my head, but if Peg reckons she needs you, then that's good enough. I'd never hear the last of it, if I sent you away.' He turned, and his last words were flung curtly over his shoulder. 'You can stay.'

He walked away, sauntering on those absurdly long legs of his, casually self assured . . . as if I were no more bother to him than the flies that had started pestering me. Two other men came across the yard and Blue Malone moved off with them. Obviously he considered me to be of no further importance. Thanks for nothing! I thought, resentfully — but at least I could stay, and that for the moment solved one of my problems.

Later, I unpacked my cases in a large, old-fashioned bedroom tucked away under the roof, a whitewashed room with a huge double bed covered by a patchwork quilt. I hung my few dresses in the carved wardrobe that could well have come out with the first settlers, and folded the rest of my belongings into the paper-lined drawers. A jubilant Peg had told me that my charge, little Jinny, was taking a nap, and so I was free to rest — but I was far too unsettled to lie down. I opened the fly-screen, and leaned out of the window. From the back of the house I looked out, not on to the grazing meadows which spread out from the front, but on to dry bush land . . . low, greeny-grey shrubs, with the occasional weird shape of a blackboy tree.

I gave a sigh of satisfaction. *This* was the Australia I had wanted to get to know . . . this wild country, its grass baked orange-gold under a burnished sky, a far cry from the flat I shared with Brian in Sydney after we had emigrated. In a strange way it filled something inside me, something that had been achingly empty. It was so vast and varied, this adopted land of mine. I had fallen in love with it, the moment I set foot on Aussie soil. Not like Brian . . .

I shut the window with a snap. It was a mistake to look back. There were some things I had to forget. I had been told that, and I knew it was good advice. Brian was one of them. Well . . . Noongarra seemed as good a place to start, as any.

I found my way down the back stairs to a bathroom. Like the rest of the house it showed surprising signs of neglect. The Malones were rich, so I had been told by a rather gossipy woman in the agency who had arranged the introduction, and indeed I could see it from the size of the house and the quality of the furniture. It was just that the original comfort was faded and dimmed, and the whole place had an uncared for, an unloved air. It seemed Peg had no more interest in the house than her brother. What, I wondered, had happened to Blue Malone's wife? Surely she would have brought a woman's touch to this otherwise lovely home.

I turned the knob, and stepped under the welcome sting of a cold shower. As I did so a memory came back to me — sudden and sharp — of my parents' home in the green countryside of Wales, clean and bright as a new pin. My mother had never been happier than when cooking or polishing. She was a small brown woman, and I took after her in looks, though not — alas — in wisdom. She had been blessed with a talent for home-making, and had ruled Dad and me with a fierce, protective love.

She hadn't been at all happy with my decision to marry Brian, a young English accountant with a ready smile, and soft clean hands. 'I know you, Megan fach,' she'd scolded. 'You need a real man, not a spoiled brat.'

The memory shattered as it trespassed on forbidden ground. I groped for a towel, and wiped eyes that were stinging. It was an ironic stroke of fate that Dad had been killed by a hit-and-run driver barely a month after Brian and I had emigrated. There hadn't been enough money left to return for the funeral . . . or so Brian had insisted. Then, as if she had lost the will to live, Mam had succumbed to bronchial pneumonia. There wasn't much point in returning then. At least, I thought bitterly, she'd not had time to discover how right she had been about Brian.

Stop it! I scowled to myself in the bathroom mirror. I mustn't let my thoughts stray in that direction . . . hadn't I learned that by now? Think of something else . . . Mr Malone, for instance.

I began drying myself vigorously, my mind flooding with new impressions. No longer painful ones . . . but disturbing in themselves. What was it about Blue Malone that made me feel so . . . so strangely insecure, so threatened?

I tried to puzzle it out, sifting through my recollections of him. Funnily enough, it wasn't his anger that disturbed me — not really. What then? I visualised, once more, the firm line of his jaw, the sun-burned face, his mouth so harsh . . . and yet in spite of his ferocity there was tenderness there, I felt sure. His hands had been gentle . . .

I threw down the towel, and leaned forward to examine my reflection carefully. What had he meant ' . . . you stand there looking like that'?

I twisted this way and that, but could see nothing very much out of the ordinary. I'm small, brown, and rounded, though I'd prefer to be tall and willowy. My face is heart-shaped and my eyes are, if anything, too round. Together with a mop of brown curls I can never do anything with, they make me look younger than my twenty-three years. And that's about it. Just a Welsh farm girl.

With a shrug I stopped thinking about it, and pulled a pair of faded blue jeans up over my hips. Then I wriggled into a white T-shirt that at least made me look healthy and tanned, ran a comb through my hair, and set off to explore.

Peg Malone was at a desk in the living-room, coping with a mountain of paper-work. She waved a cheerful hand at me, but was so obviously busy that I didn't like to disturb her. I was lucky to have some spare time in which to find my way around, and there was plenty to see outside.

Near the house jasmine, bottle brush and kangaroo paws gave welcome shade from the afternoon sun, but — as if drawn by the memory of our last encounter — I braved the heat that rose from the dusty surface of the yard, and crossed to where I had last seen Blue. I climbed the white fence that divided the yard from the paddock, and sat astride its top rail, looking out across the stretch of sun-baked meadows that ended at the horizon in a low line of trees.

At the far end of the paddock a group of men were moving sheep through a gap into the next field. I looked to see if I could spot Blue's unmistakable head, but there was no sign of him. Perhaps he was too important to take part in the manual work . . . but no. Instinctively I knew that this would not be so. Wealthy he must be, the owner of this whole spread, but Patrick Malone had the stamp of a man who knew what it was like to work hard and would drive others to do the same. I vowed to myself that he would have no cause for complaint with *my* work.

One of the workers began strolling across the field. He was making directly for me, peeling off his shirt as he walked, revealing a smooth, deeply-tanned chest.

When he reached me he treated me to a lazy smile, teeth gleaming, eyes large and liquid in a swarthy face.

'G'day . . . so you're the Pommie girl that's workin' here?'

My answering glance was cool, but I hoped, not unfriendly. 'I'm Megan Roberts, if that's what you mean.'

His glance slid over me, registering approval. 'You're only a little scrap, aren't you . . . to be a Jillaroo?'

I must have looked puzzled, because he chuckled and leaned against the fence, closer to me. 'I forgot you wouldn't understand. Jillaroo . . . that's a sort of female apprentice here.'

'I see.' Jillaroo! Well, I'd wanted to do something different. It looked as though I'd had my wish.

He tilted his head, and gave me a slow, meaningful smile. 'Blue must be hard put to it, if he needs a Sheila to help out . . . or perhaps that isn't what he wants you for?'

I could see he was teasing me, and refused to swallow the bait. 'I've been hired to help with the house and the little girl,' I said calmly. 'I don't somehow think I'll be expected to shear the sheep, Mr . . . er?'

'Craig Morelli. Craig to you, sweetheart. I'm top hand here.'

The Italian surname explained the dark good looks. Though he sounded as Australian as they came — probably a second or third generation immigrant. I didn't much like his brash approach, but I'd been in Australia long enough to understand their easy-going ways, and at least he was sociable, which was more than could be said for his boss. It occurred to me that I might find myself glad of a friendly face.

'As a matter of fact it was Mr Malone's sister who hired me,' I told him.

'Peg?' He rolled a cigarette deftly, and bent his head to light it. 'She's all right, is Peg. Broke her leg a bit back . . . that's why she needs help, though I reckon it's a good excuse for her. She's never been one for housework. She'd rather be out, helping the lads.'

He smiled at me intimately, moving closer. 'Think you'll like it here?'

'Oh yes!' I had no doubts on that score. I loved this country. After Brian had left me, and even throughout the traumatic time that followed, the thought of quitting had never once entered my head.

Craig slid an arm casually around my waist, at the same time pointing to the horizon where a thin spiral of smoke rose into the air as straight as a line drawn with a ruler.

'Bush fire.'

I stiffened — at his actions more than

his words — and disengaging myself, shifted farther along the fence. 'Isn't that dangerous?' I asked, choosing to ignore his familiarity.

He looked amused at my retreat, and shrugged. 'Not really. You see them all the time in the dry season. Just a bit of bush burning. We can keep them under control.'

'Is it a very big farm?'

He snorted with laughter. 'This is a sheep station, sweetheart — not a farm. Sure — it's one of the biggest round about. A good few thousand merinos, at any rate.' His face lit up at an idea. 'Say — why don't I show you around? Can you ride?'

'Well . . . yes,' I answered doubtfully. It seemed an age since I'd last sat astride the little pony I'd known since childhood. But why not? I was dying to know Noongarra better, and pushy though Craig was I didn't doubt that I could handle him.

'You don't think Mr Malone would mind?'

Craig gave me a sideways glance, and grinned. 'Why should he mind? Doubt if he'll even notice you're gone. A woman-hater he is. Not like me now. I'm right glad to see you . . . you'll sure brighten up my days.'

I avoided the challenge of his eyes. 'Well then,' I said with deliberate prim politeness. 'That would be very nice. Thank you.'

'Craig!'

My heart plummetted to my sandals. There was no mistaking that voice. I turned, to see the tall figure of Blue Malone stalking towards us. Craig moved away from me. He dropped his cigarette, grinding it carefully underfoot. 'I was just about to take Megan here for a ride, to show her the ropes,' he began.

'Very thoughtful of you. But I'd rather you got back to your work.'

The steel in Blue's voice brooked no argument, and Craig sloped off after giving me a defiant wink which I pretended not to notice. A strong hand fastened around my arm, and I was hurried towards the house.

'I've a few words to say to you, young lady,' he ground out through clenched teeth. 'You said you'd be no trouble, and yet the moment my back's turned you're flirting with the hired hands.'

'I'm what!'

'You heard.' He walked with such long, quick strides that I found I was running by his side, unable to free myself. His grip was painful. We reached the verandah before I could break loose.

'How dare you!' I ran up the steps ahead of him, and spun round to look down. The harsh lines of his face were set, but the extra height made me bold . . . it was easier, I found, to be aggressive when you towered over someone. 'Craig was only being helpful and polite . . . '

'Craig isn't paid to dance attendance on you. He has better things to do.' His voice was curt, his eyes hard and unfriendly. 'I'll thank you not to entice my hands away from their work.'

I could hardly believe he was serious. People just didn't talk like that these days. 'Now look here . . . '

He pushed past me. 'I knew a woman would cause trouble. If you cause it like this wherever you go I'm not surprised your husband left you.'

It was too much! Like a small thunderbolt I shot ahead of him once more, barring his way.

'And what do you mean by that? You know nothing about me.'

'I hardly need to,' he countered coldly. 'I can see enough to guess you kept the men running after you. Dare say that was the trouble . . . a man wouldn't walk out on a woman for nothing.'

'A lot you know about it! I've just about had enough of you and your clever remarks. What gives you the right to sit in judgment on me?' I was shaking with anger, wishing . . . no, longing . . . in some way to pierce his solid armour of indifference. 'Just who d'you think you are, suggesting I encouraged men?' My scorn reached boiling point. 'Not that they'd have run after me, the way . . . the way I was . . . '

I stopped abruptly, all the fight draining out of me. The old misery came flooding up in a grey wave, engulfing me . . . and I'd been fool enough to think I had it under control . . .

'What d'you mean?'

I wrenched him back into focus. He was looking at me as if he was seeing me as a real person for the first time — but I shook my head blindly. I was past caring now. 'Nothing,' I muttered. 'It doesn't matter.'

'If you're to look after the child, it matters to me,' he insisted. 'What was wrong with you? You can't start sentences and not finish them.'

'Can't I?' A little of my fighting spirit returned. 'Just watch me . . . I'm an expert at it.'

He shook his head, an expression of exasperation crossing his face. 'You still owe me an explanation.'

'I owe you nothing!' I couldn't think why he was persisting. His probing was like a knife turning in old wounds. These were memories I had come so far to escape. Memories I had thought to have buried for ever, but he was forcing me to face them again. And still he stood there, obviously expecting an answer. At that moment I hated him more than anyone . . . even Brian.

'I think perhaps I'd better leave, after all, Mr Malone,' I said woodenly.

His lips moved, but I couldn't hear his reply for the roaring in my ears. His face began to recede. And then, just as my knees were about to buckle, I found myself in his arms again. My instinct was to fight him off — but somehow it felt so good . . . so safe. With a tiny sigh, I relaxed, my cheek against his shoulder, my curls tucked under his chin as he carried me like a baby.

'Peg!' I heard him call, as he elbowed his way through the door. 'Call Melody to give us a hand. I seem to be making a habit of this!'

2

'Are you feeling better?' Peg's worried face hung in front of me. For a moment I couldn't think why she should look so concerned, then it dawned on me what was wrong. I was lying on that darned sofa again!

I raised myself on an elbow. 'What . . . what happened?'

Another face swam into view; the dark features and spread-out nostrils of an aboriginal woman this time. 'You all right?' it echoed.

'Of *course* she is, Melody. She only came over dizzy.'

I remembered then — the cruelly insistent questions, and my own unexpected urge to relax . . . to give way to the illusion of safety in the arms of a man who had already spelled out what he thought of me. I tried to twist around. 'Where . . . ?'

'I'm here.' Anticipating my question, he moved into view and stood looking down on me with a faint frown.

'D'you think we should get the Doc?' Peg asked.

'I c'n ring the Clinic.' Melody's teeth flashed, eagerly helpful.

Patrick Malone ran a hand through his hair. 'Calm down, will you both? Strewth, how women do flap.' He scowled. 'You've only to look at her to see she's fit as a flea. A healthier specimen I've never seen.'

Taken aback, I was caught by an unexpected giggle, which somehow turned into a hiccup. 'You make me sound like one of your sheep.'

'A sheep'd have more sense.' He gave a resigned sigh, and sat at the end of the sofa. 'OK then . . . tell me, when did you last eat?'

'Eat?' I echoed. It was the last thing I expected him to say.

'Yes, eat. You know . . . you open your mouth and put in food, and . . . '

'No need — hic — to be sarcastic.'

'So? Will you answer my question, or is it something else you don't choose to talk about?'

I turned pink. There *had* been food available on the long train crossing of the Nullabor, but I had been conscious of my dwindling resources. He made me feel on trial — a naughty child.

'I — hic — wasn't hungry,' I lied, trying to muster up some dignity.

He made a sound of disgust. 'I thought so. All through that heat, and nothing in her stomach. It's a wonder she made it this far.'

'Food's all ready,' Melody offered. 'I was just goin' to fetch little Jinny, and then dish it up.'

'Thank goodness for that,' Blue said, rising. 'I'm starving. As for this young woman, perhaps if we feed her she'll stop looking like a badly treated koala and give me some peace. Come on!' He caught hold of my hands and pulled me up. 'I'll take you to your room. At least you'll be out from under my feet there.'

What was the use of protesting . . . he

wouldn't pay any attention. I had neither physical nor moral strength enough to resist him. Besides which, I thought with resignation as he hoisted me up once more, I was beginning to get used to being carted around.

Peg hovered. 'Are you sure she'll be all right? This *is* a nuisance . . . I was hoping . . . '

Blue swung around, making the room spin dizzily. I clasped him around his neck, to steady myself.

'Hoping what?' he demanded. 'What are you up to now, Peg?'

'Oh nothing — nothing.' His sister's face was a picture of innocence. 'Take her up Blue, I've put her in your old room. I'll send up her dinner in a moment.'

'Thank you, Peg,' I called defiantly over Blue's shoulder, as he carried me out of the room. 'But please don't worry about me . . . truly there's *nothing* wrong.' Nothing — except that my heart was still pounding at twice its normal rate.

'I — hic — I'm not too heavy for you, am I?' I asked pointedly.

He took a tighter grip around my waist, and made a noise that sounded suspiciously like a chuckle.

'Last time I carried something your weight, it was a fat old ewe,' he remarked. 'Only she had a better temper.'

I peered into his face. 'You're laughing!' I accused, with a strange leaping of my pulse.

'Me? Perish the thought.' He stopped for a moment and turned his head. It made me giddy, to have his eyes looking so closely into mine. I thought for a moment that I had surprised in him quite a different expression, but he dropped me without ceremony on to my feet at the bedroom door.

'Quite sure you can manage now?' The sarcasm was back.

I reddened. 'Of course.' Trust him to make it sound as if it had been *my* idea to be carried. I turned with relief to the sanctuary of my room, but even there I wasn't safe. He followed me in. I scuttled on to the vast bed, and curled up defensively. Was he going to continue his questioning, even here? But he wasn't paying me any attention. He was looking around the room, almost as if he had never seen it before.

'Peg said this was your old room,' I ventured at last.

'Yes.'

He offered no further comment, but wandered across to the window, staring out. It was obviously a double-room. I waited. Then, as the silence dragged on

' . . . was that when . . . ?'

'My wife was alive? Yes.'

His tone was noncommital, almost as though it had been a matter of no importance. But it answered one of the things that had been puzzling me. Thinking aloud I murmured, 'Jinny is nearly four, I believe . . . '

'And that makes it nearly four years since my wife died.'

He swung around, and leaned back on the deep window-ledge, his arms folded, eyes bleak. 'Does that quench your curiosity?'

My chin went up. 'I wasn't . . . '

He shrugged. 'Don't apologise. Let's get the details over, saves time that way. Francesca died soon after Jinny was born. There had been complications. And I'm *not* looking for another wife. Satisfied?'

The sun pouring through the window behind him lit up his hair and spilled over the sharp angle of his jaw and across the broad width of his shoulders. With a tightening in my stomach, I had to admit the strength of the attraction this man held, even while his manner made my hackles rise.

'Do you have to be so disagreeable?' I retorted. 'I wasn't being nosey. Not any more than you were with me. Two can ask questions you know.'

To my surprise his stern features broke into a smile. It warmed his eyes, softened the line of his mobile mouth, made him something approaching human.

'I'm sorry. We both seem to have dark areas we're touchy about.'

Dark areas! What a perfect description. It was as if he knew all about me . . . could see into the depths of my soul.

'I can promise you, I'm not trying to hide anything. Only . . . some things . . . I just can't face yet.'

He merely nodded, back to his sombre expression, and turned to go.

'Wait! Mr Malone, I'm getting a little confused . . . does this mean I'm staying, after all?'

He opened the door, then paused and shrugged. 'Seems to me it was your decision to leave — not mine. I don't go back on my word. Now, for pity's sake, can't you stop being so formal? I'm usually called Blue.'

I relaxed. Would I ever know where I stood with my employer? One minute he was being disagreeable . . . the next, well . . . *almost* nice to me. 'Does that mean you've changed your opinion of me?' I asked hopefully.

He looked at me in cold surprise. 'Don't get me wrong, young lady. I've said you can stay — that's all. I'm not obliged to approve of you, and I'll be keeping a close eye on what you get up to.'

He started out of the room.

My eyes narrowed, and my lips tightened. 'Pig!' I muttered.

There was a silence outside, then he wandered back, framed in the doorway.

'Yes?' I said, round eyed.

The look he gave me was wary. He cleared his throat. 'Hmmph! Your hiccups seem to have stopped.' Then he left. This time he really *had* gone, I could hear his footsteps receding.

I chuckled. Somehow he didn't frighten me as much as he had. It was no use getting angry with him, he was used to his sister fighting back, and could deal with that. Better to act sweet . . . if he really was a woman-hater he would keep his distance.

'Dinner's up.' Melody bustled in

without knocking, a tray held out before her.

A small child was clutching at her skirts, a mere scrap — bare feet and dusty thin legs, dark eyes peering from beneath tangled black curls. She was so dark that for a second I assumed she must be one of Melody's offspring — and then the penny dropped.

'Jinny?' I asked softly, as I took the tray.

'C'mon,' Melody said. 'Say 'lo to the lady.'

I smiled, as the child retreated behind the broad beam of the aboriginal woman. 'Hello there,' I coaxed. 'I've come to look after you. D'you think you'll like that?'

A cautious head peeped out. The dark eyes examined me, then the little face was lit by a flashing smile.

'Yis!'

The excitement proved too much, and the small body hurtled out of the door, bare feet pattering away.

Melody chuckled. 'She's goin' to bed

in a minute . . . after her bath.'

I felt guilty. 'But surely I ought to be doing that, not just sitting here being waited on. I should tuck her up . . . or perhaps her father . . . ?'

Melody flapped a broad palm. 'Na . . . Mr Blue don't go near. You sit there and eat your food. I'll see to her tonight. Can't have you passin' out again. You cin start work in the mornin'.'

Obediently I took a mouthful. Mutton stew — predictable enough on a sheep station, I supposed, but it was tasty and hot. I really *was* hungry.

Melody showed no eagerness to leave. 'Lots of things for you to do here,' she remarked. 'You like sewin'?'

'Well . . . it depends.' I had never been one to make a lot of clothes. High fashion had not interested me. 'What kind of sewing?'

'Curtains,' Melody said. She folded her arms, and her face crinkled into a broad smile. 'There's a stack of material in the chest downstairs. Been there since Mrs Malone bought it 'fore Jinny was born, and nobody's touched it since. Miss Peg — she's no hand at sewin', and the place needs seeing to. And Jinny now ... she needs new clothes. Most times she's playin' out back in the dirt in nothing but her panties. T'aint really right.'

'I think I could manage that,' I answered. 'Jinny's a pretty little thing. Is her name short for ... ?'

'Gina. Named after her granny on her mother's side. Francesca ... that was Mrs Malone ... her parents still run the vineyard.'

'Are they Italian then?' I remembered the man I had met earlier. 'I met an Italian here today ... '

'Craig. Second cousin. Most of the vineyards just south of here are run by Italians. They stick together mostly, but there's not enough work for them all in the vineyards, so you'll find plenty on the spreads round about. Francesca's brother used to live here, too ... but he's bin gone to some kind of college to learn about the vines. He'll take over from his parents one day.'

'What was Mrs Malone — Francesca — like?' I asked with some diffidence. I didn't want to be thought prying, but Melody had no objection to feeding my curiosity.

'Most pretty thing you ever saw,' she said with a sigh. 'Jinny's the spittin' image of her.'

I recalled the vivid little face, the bright shy eyes. I could well imagine those looks developing into real beauty in a woman. And yet Patrick Malone was a woman-hater? Why should that be?

Melody continued. 'Mr Blue — he adored her. Worshipped the ground she walked on. But I reckon he sensed somethin' was goin' to happen, 'cos from the moment she became pregnant he became very quiet . . . moody. Then when she died he just froze up somehow . . . never shed a tear.'

Well — that answered my unspoken question. How sad . . . and yet perhaps it *hadn't* really answered it . . . why should losing the wife he adored make Blue Malone hate all other women? Perhaps, I mused, he resents the fact that we are still alive.

'Is there anythin' else you'd like?' Melody asked. 'I've apple pie, if you'd care for it?'

I shook my head, and pushed away my empty plate. 'I couldn't eat another mouthful,' I said truthfully. I snuggled down on the pillows, and before I knew it, I was asleep.

I didn't sleep for long, and once I woke I began to wonder what I should do next. It had been a very strange day, but I felt perfectly fit now, and I could hardly sit about all evening. After debating the problem for some time I decided to rejoin the family.

Downstairs I found Peg seated at her desk once more, this time speaking on the telephone. Seeing me, she stopped and waved me towards a door at the far end of the room. 'Go into the sitting-room, dear. Blue's waiting for you.'

He was lounging in a deep armchair which faced the door — as if he had been lying in wait for me.

I licked my lips nervously as I met his unwavering stare.

'What's my sister up to out there?'

His abrupt question startled me. 'What d'you mean? Peg's on the phone, I believe.'

His brows drew into a straight disapproving line. 'Hatching something, if I know her. D'you know what it's about?'

'I don't listen to other people's conversations,' I retorted. 'If you want to know, why don't you go out there and hear for yourself?' Darn it! I'd done it again — let him get under my skin. I perched on the edge of a chair, willing myself to look relaxed.

'Hmmm.' His eyes left my face, and dropped to examine the rest of me, travelling slowly down to the curve of my hip on the chair, the way I was sitting making my skirt tight across the line of my thigh. Perhaps he thought I had chosen to sit that way, to be provocative. I jumped up.

'What . . . what a lovely room this is,' I stammered, on the pretext of looking at one of the gilt-framed pictures that hung on the far wall.

'What was Craig planning to do with you?'

I swung around. 'I beg your pardon?'

A sarcastic grin crossed his face. 'I'll re-phrase that. What I meant was, where was he aiming to take you?'

'Oh.' I decided not to press the point. 'He was just going to show me around the estate.'

He quirked an eyebrow. 'You're really interested?'

'Yes, of course I am.' My voice lifted indignantly. 'What d'you think? That I only came here to look for men?' *Gently. Cool it.* I took a calming breath. 'I can't wait to get to know this place. It must give you a great thrill, to think your family started it, and here you are still, carrying it on.'

He sat silently for a while, as if digesting what I had said. Then he rose to his feet. 'Come on, then.'

'Come? Come where?'

'To have a look around. If you really want to.'

I glanced down at my dress. 'But I'm not ready for riding.'

'We'll drive,' he said impatiently. 'It'll be quicker, if we want to get around while there's still light. I'll look you out a mount tomorrow, if you want to ride.'

He took my agreement for granted, and I followed him back through the family-room where his sister was still on the phone. Peg stopped talking as we arrived, and Blue cast her an inquiring glance. Was he always so suspicious — even of his own sister? I wondered. What could it possibly matter to him who Peg was talking to, or about what? It was surely nobody's business but her own.

I glanced at him, as I took my place beside him in the powerful utility vehicle the Aussies call a ute.

As we drove he explained that the grazing we were passing were known as the Windrow Meadows. It was this area that had been granted to his forebears when they had first emigrated from Ireland.

'It was hard going,' he commented laconically, 'but they survived.'

I guessed it was an understatement. I could imagine the struggles of the hardy folk who had battled their way through hardship to the prosperity he now enjoyed. Though he had to battle still, I supposed, if he was to keep it. I became so interested that I forgot to be wary, and plied him with excited questions which he answered with good humoured patience.

We moved on, and on either side of me I could see stretching for miles the grassland that supported the thick-woolled merino sheep. I became dazed with the names he tossed at me, Ram Paddock, Middle Paddock, Rocky Ridge, Hoggets Paddock, The Lagoon. I had thought the land to be flat, but I was mistaken. It rose to quite a steep ridge, topped by the trees, then dipped steeply into thickly wooded scrubland.

'Where's this lagoon you mentioned,' I asked, as we jolted and juddered into it. 'That sounds like water — but everything looks as dry as a bone.'

'You're right. That's what it's like now, but in the rainy season it's a different matter.'

Suddenly we came to a clearing, and the remains of a lake. The water level was down now, and it was edged by caked and cracked mud, but there was still a little water in the bottom. Blue stopped the ute, and turned off the engine. 'This is what I wanted you to hear,' he said. 'Let's get out.'

'To hear? Whatever do you mean?'

But as I followed him, I realised what he meant. The air was vibrating. He turned to me, smiling. 'And what d'you think that is?'

I listened. The sound was made up of hundreds of smaller sounds, melodious, as if a thousand strings were being plucked at once.

'Frogs?' I ventured.

'Right on. Banjo frogs, they're called. They sound off at this time of the evening, just as night falls. I thought you'd like to hear them.'

'What will happen if this lagoon dries up completely?' I asked.

He shrugged. 'I've never known it to happen yet. There's always a little water left, and when the rains come you'd be surprised. You get flash floods here. Look . . . ' He pointed across to the far side, where a huge pipe was sticking out of the bank. 'You'd never think a pipe that size was needed for drainage, would you? But believe me, it is. All the other side of the lagoon becomes a swamp in the wet.'

'And what's over there? When you come out of the trees, I mean.'

'More meadows. More sheep.'

'And still Noongarra?'

'Still ours.'

It certainly made me think. I was

used to the sheep on the bare slopes of Moel Famau. That had seemed spacious enough to me . . . but this was sheep farming on quite a different scale.

'We'd better be getting back,' he said. 'It'll be dark in a jiffy.'

As we turned back to the car I stumbled, and he put a steadying hand under my arm. How different he seemed. Perhaps he was already regretting the frosty reception he had given me.

'Mr Malone . . . Blue,' I said tentatively. 'Thank you for bringing me. And . . . I'm sorry if I was taking Craig away from his work. He offered, and I just didn't think . . .'

He reached out to open the car door for me, but hesitated, looking down at me. 'No . . . that's your trouble. You don't think . . . do you? I wasn't bothered about the time wasted.'

'What then?' The criticism was back in his voice, and I bridled.

He heaved a sigh. 'Maybe things are

different in the city. But here . . . well, didn't it occur to you that accepting a stranger's invitation to wander off into the wilderness with him might be misconstrued ..?'

I looked at him with amazement, and laughed scornfully. 'Oh come on . . . And in any case, I'm a big girl now. I could handle Craig.'

'Could you?' He opened the car door, but as I moved forward to get into it, he suddenly caught me by the arms. The next minute I was crushed against him, and his mouth was on mine, taking my breath away.

Then, just as suddenly, he let go of me, and we stood staring at one another. I just didn't know what to say, and he scowled. 'Still think you could take care of yourself? Maybe Craig wouldn't have stopped at a kiss.'

Angrily I pushed past him and climbed into the ute. 'It seems to me, Mr Malone, that you shouldn't expect other people to behave as badly as yourself,' I hissed. 'I'm sure Craig would have treated me with more respect than you have. And I'll make friends with whoever I like.'

'Hmmph!' He made no further comment, and I sat stiffly beside him as we drove back. I stared fixedly out of the car window, though it was now getting too dark to see anything much.

Truth to tell, I was more angry with myself than with him. So he had been trying to teach me a lesson, had he? That was his excuse. But I had no excuse. None at all. I should have kicked, or bit him . . . or . . . or, well *something*. Instead of which I had found myself responding.

'Here we are,' he said, breaking the long silence, and I realised we had reached the house without my noticing it, so engrossed had I been in my own thoughts. I stalked in ahead of him, letting him see that I was still angry.

Peg met us as though we had been away for weeks.

'So there you are! I've been waiting for you, to tell you . . . '

'Tell us what Peg?' Blue demanded. 'I knew you were up to something.'

She grinned all over her pleasant face. 'Nothing very terrible. You know my friend Maisie's girl is getting married in Perth? Well, she wanted me to go up there with them, and stay a while. Of course I couldn't . . . not the way things were. But now . . . '

'You mean you've fixed up to go . . . without telling me?'

'Well — you wouldn't want to spoil my fun, would you? And I'm not much use to you like this.' She turned to me. 'You can manage, Megan, can't you?'

I was only just beginning to take in all the implications. *No!* I wanted to shout, but how could I when she looked so pleased, and no doubt she needed the break. 'I . . . Oh, yes . . . I can manage.'

'There!' She looked triumphantly at her brother. 'Maisie's picking me up first thing in the morning. I'm glad you two are getting on OK. It'll give you time to get to know one another.'

She swung off on her crutches, to do

her packing, leaving me standing awkwardly, wondering what on earth to say. Was I being stupid, taking a kiss so seriously?

'Trust Peg to arrange something like this!' Blue exploded. 'Women!'

He sounded so disgusted that I had to smile. 'I expect we'll manage,' I ventured.

His blue eyes looked at me fiercely. 'I *knew* you'd be trouble.'

'Well!' I gasped. 'I like that! You can't blame me for this.'

'If you hadn't been here, she wouldn't be going.' He thought a minute. 'Well, I guess she deserves it, at that.' He wagged a finger in my direction. 'Just so long as you watch your step. Do as I say, and don't distract the men.'

'Really . . . '

I turned on my heel and left him. Just who did he think he was? I was fuming . . . and yet later that night, when I lay in the soft bed under the patchwork quilt I couldn't stop thinking about the way it had felt to be in his arms.

3

The next morning things didn't seem quite so bad — they never do after a good night's sleep, I'd noticed that before — and I *had* slept well, like a log in fact.

It was early, but I got up, anyway. I was used to life on a farm, and knew that people would already be out and about. A quick glance from the window proved me right.

After I had dressed — once more in jeans and Tee shirt — I went along to Jinny's room. The child was still asleep, a little curled up bundle, the bedclothes thrown off, one arm flung above her head.

I made a quick investigation of Jinny's cupboards and drawers, to see what she should wear that day. When I finally pulled out a pair of red shorts and a blouse, I was looking thoughtful.

Melody had been right. I wouldn't say that Jinny's wardrobe was poverty-stricken . . . what clothes she did have were expensive and well made. But . . . they were all shorts or dungarees. Where were all the pretty things that little girls love to wear on special occasions?

By the time I had sorted out her underwear, of which there was a singular lack, Jinny had woken up.

'Hello, Jinny,' I said cheerfully. 'I'm Megan. And I'm awfully hungry. Suppose I help you get dressed, then you can show me what we have for breakfast.'

Slowly she climbed out of her bed and, intrigued, began to struggle into the clothes I handed her. She was a capable little thing, but now and again she needed a steadying hand, and gradually she overcame her shyness and leaned against me. I put my arm around her waist. She felt light and warm, like a small bird.

'I'll brush your hair,' I said. 'It's very pretty hair.'

She peered at me through her ebony locks as I ran the comb along the crown of her head to make a parting. 'So's yours,' she whispered huskily.

My laugh was a little shaky. 'Well, thank you Jinny. Now . . . let's go, shall we?'

She led me down into a vast kitchen, where Melody was busy washing up the crocks.

'Men've fed,' she informed us. 'Sit you down . . . what'll you have?'

At that hour all I wanted was fruit juice, cold and fresh from the huge old fridge that stood in one corner, and toast with butter and marmalade. Jinny had a bowl of cereal, spooning it up quickly, her bright eyes never leaving my face.

'Is Peg about?' I asked.

'Yes . . . indeed I am, my dear!' Peg came swinging into the kitchen on those crutches of hers. She managed them very well. I was beginning to think she quite enjoyed them.

'I'm all packed,' she said cheerfully. 'Bless you, Megan. You can't think how

I'm looking forward to this visit. Maisie'll be coming for me any moment now. Is there anything you want to ask, before I go?'

'Er . . . ' I was sure there were a million things, but on the spur of the moment they all flew out of my head. 'I don't think so,' I said weakly. 'I'll manage. Have a nice time.'

'Oh, I will. I will.' There was the blare of a horn from outside. 'There they are!' she said excitedly. She kissed Jinny. 'Now be a good girl for Megan.' She turned to me. 'Oh, I forgot. There's some money on the sideboard, if you need anything. But Blue will see you right. Tell him if you're short.'

Then she went loping out, hopping down the verandah steps, and Melody and I carried her cases out to the waiting station wagon. She had two large ones, and I began to wonder how long she intended to stay away.

'Goodbye. Goodbye,' we all called, and Jinny waved her thin arms frantically above her head, and ran behind the car laughing and whooping, as far as the gate to Noongarra. There was no sign of Blue.

When Jinny came running back to me I looked at her doubtfully. 'And what am I to do with you, young lady? Do you want to play outside, or would you like to work with me?'

'Work with you,' she said with no hesitation, and it seemed as if I had made a conquest.

I offered to give Melody a hand in the kitchen, but she left me in no doubt that that was her domain, and she could manage on her own, so I decided to start on the house. I discovered a vacuum cleaner, and made a start with that. It wasn't too difficult, because the floor was of narrow pine strips, covered with rugs, and these I dragged out and hung over a line at the back of the house. I found a nice long stick, and left Jinny beating the living daylights out of them, while I set to work on the floor.

This took us half the morning, and we were glad to stop and take the elevenses Melody brought us, coffee for me and milk for Jinny, and golden pumpkin scones straight out of the oven. We ate them sitting on the verandah steps. It was there that Blue found us.

He was only passing, but he stopped and cast a cold eye over us.

'Taking life easily?' he enquired.

I bit into a scone, and refrained from answering.

Jinny wasn't so restrained. 'Daddy . . . we've had all the rugs up,' she chattered eagerly. 'An' Megan hung them out the back. An' I beat them with a big stick. An' Megan's polished the floor, and made it shine . . . an' Daddy . . . won't you come an' look?'

To his credit he did look a bit uncomfortable, but what he did then made my blood boil. Jinny in her excitement had leaped up and grabbed him by his arm. He just untangled her fingers, and put her from him without even a smile of acknowledgment. 'Later,' he said without emotion, and moved on.

Jinny's lower lip quivered, but she said nothing. She just came back and climbed up on the step beside me, and buried her face in her glass of milk.

'Daddy's very busy,' I said gently. She looked up, a white moustache on her top lip. 'He'll see later on,' I continued. 'In any case, we haven't finished yet. We've got to make the furniture shine. I'll find you a duster.'

Her disappointment forgotten she scampered in with me, and we set to with a will, cleaning and polishing for all we were worth. I attacked the big carved sideboard in what was known as the family-room, taking out on it all the disapproval I felt for its owner. What a way to speak to a child! Didn't he care for Jinny at all?

By lunch-time we had finished, in that room at any rate. There were other things I wanted to do . . . the curtains, for instance, and maybe some cushion covers to match . . . but for now the room looked a hundred times better, shining and welcoming, and smelling of polish.

I sent Jinny to wash her hands, and stood back to see what we had achieved. I had a pleasant feeling of satisfaction. It was a long time since I had had anything resembling a home. When we left Wales Brian had insisted on leaving everything behind, and once we arrived at Sydney he seemed unable to settle. We kept moving from one apartment to another, and everywhere we went he grumbled and blamed everyone else for his lack of success.

I had managed to get a job as a receptionist. I hadn't particularly liked it, but it helped, and I hoped that in a little while we would be able to afford a home of our own. I kept telling myself Brian would change, once he settled down. Well . . . he did change, but not in the way I expected.

I shook my head angrily, forcing away the painful memories, and went to prepare myself for lunch. Jinny and I had it with Melody, the men having taken theirs with them to eat wherever they might be that day. They would all return in the evening for a good substantial meal.

'What you gonna do this afternoon?' Melody asked, after Jinny had disappeared to her room for a nap.

'I don't know. I found a sewing machine this morning, in that cupboard under the stairs. But I need cottons, and some new needles; the ones in it are all rusted. And I could make some dresses for Jinny ... but I'd need materials and a pattern.'

'It's the child's birthday on Sunday,' she said with a quick glance at me out of her shrewd black eyes.

I was dumbfounded. Jinny's *birthday!* Why didn't someone tell me? How could Peg go away ... what about presents? I looked at her warily. 'Has Mr Malone got a present for her?' I asked casually.

She shrugged her big shoulders, and crinkled up her nose, making it look flatter than ever. 'Dunno. I'll make a cake. Can't say more than that.'

My resentment of my employer flared

up stronger than ever. Didn't he care for his daughter at all? Grief stricken about his wife he may be, but there was no need to take it out on an innocent child. It made my blood boil. And what was I to do? I should have a present for her. I wondered if I could get into town some time during the week.

As it happened, the opportunity presented itself almost immediately. Craig came into the kitchen, walking in with that hint of a swagger in his walk.

'I'm goin' into Bunbury for oats. Anything you want?'

I jumped to my feet. 'Yes . . . will you take me? I have a little shopping to do, if it won't delay you.' I was conscious of his boss's warning, and didn't want to be accused of keeping him from his duties.

The smile he flashed me was full of bravado, as if he cared nothing for Blue's displeasure, which I knew was not the case. 'Take all the time you want.'

Melody said she didn't mind keeping

an eye on Jinny if she was about before I got back, so I ran upstairs and grabbed my purse and a light denim jacket, and soon I was beside Craig in the truck, rattling along to the town.

It was hot in the truck, and I was glad I'd had the sense to cover up my arms. Even with the windows wound down it seemed airless, and the sun burned in on me. Craig pointed out to me the boundaries of the Noongarra property and told me something about the properties that adjoined Blue's, and the time passed quickly until we drew up in the town. Then he looked at me a little dubiously, and I could tell he was wondering what to do with me.

'I'll find my own way around,' I said quickly. I had no wish to have him tagging around with me. 'I'll meet you here again in . . . say half an hour. Or is that too long?'

He assured me that his business would take him at least that, and so I was free. I really enjoyed that half hour. I didn't dare venture too far, there wasn't time, but I saw enough to like the town. Although quite a busy place, it still, to me, had a feel of the West about it. It was clean and fresh, and the arcaded sidewalks of Victoria Street, dominated by the spire and red roofs of St Patrick's Cathedral intrigued me.

I soon found what I wanted. I bought a few personal things for myself, and then discovered a small shop in an arcade that sold cottons. After that I counted my money, and decided on what to get Jinny for her birthday. I ended up with a sweet little dress, but she needed other, less fancy, ones, too. I chose two lengths of material and I found an easy pattern I thought I could manage.

After that, I leaned against one of the pillars of the sidewalk, and watched the world go by while I waited for Craig. One day I would come here again, and really explore, but for now I delighted in reading the colourful shop signs, 'Asian Emporium', 'Grog', 'Crab Cooking Facilities in Beer Garden'. The place had character, in spite of the fact that none of it was really old . . .

'Are you ready then? Got what you wanted?'

Craig had returned, and was obviously wanting to be off, it was quite a long drive to Noongarra. I was quite happy to climb into the truck with my parcels. A part of my mind was already looking forward to seeing Jinny's face when she saw her dress. I hoped it would fit . . . I was sure it would . . .

The journey back was uneventful but it was just my luck, to spoil things, that Blue was in the yard as we drove up. The look on his face boded no good, though I couldn't see why. His objections to my wasting his hands' time didn't hold good this time, and he could hardly suggest I was in any moral danger in the middle of Bunbury. I grabbed my parcels and climbed down, determined to get my say in first.

He stalked towards us on his long legs, his lean face set and his eyes steely, and Craig grabbed a sack of oats from the back of the truck and beat a retreat. I stood my ground.

'Before you say anything,' I began, trying not to look as though I was quaking in my shoes. 'I did not waste any of Craig's time. Not one minute of it.'

He sighed, and ran a distracted hand through his coppery hair. 'And what about *your* time? I thought you were hired to look after the child . . . '

That stung me, and all the anger I had felt earlier came bubbling up. '*Your* child, Mr Malone,' I said stiffly. 'She does happen to have a name, you know. And I had to go into town to buy her some clothes. Did you know she hardly has a thing to wear?'

He looked astounded. 'I didn't realise . . . '

'No,' I said scathingly. 'I'm quite sure. You hardly take the time to notice the poor little mite, let alone know what's going on with her. I bet you didn't even remember it's her birthday on Sunday. It isn't fair. After all . . . it's not her fault . . . '

The colour seemed to drain from his face before my very eyes, and he took a step towards me, looking so threatening that I stepped back away from him. 'What the hell do you mean?'

'W . . . well . . . ' I stammered. 'I know you loved your wife. And it's tragic that she died having Jinny. I can understand that. I can see how you feel. But you shouldn't take it out on your daughter. She's alive, and she needs your love . . . she needs . . . '

'I don't need you to tell me what she needs.' He was furious. I quailed in front of him. 'What do *you* know about it?' he went on, his lips twisting in a snarl. 'Are you an expert? Have *you* got a child, *Mrs* Roberts?'

'No . . . ' I whispered hoarsely. 'I don't have a child, Mr Malone. I lost the child I so badly wanted, when my husband left. I was seven months pregnant at the time. I had my baby, but she didn't live.'

I couldn't say any more, the words stuck in my throat, but no tears came. I think I had cried them all, a long time ago.

It was as if time stood still, then Blue closed his eyes and groaned. 'Oh my God . . . '

What he would have said next I never knew. I was vaguely aware that one of the men was riding across the yard, and I didn't want him to hear any of this, so I turned to go into the house.

But then Jinny came out on the verandah, and saw us standing there.

'Megan . . . you're back.' She shrieked with delight, and came bounding down the steps. The next moment she was rushing like a little whirlwind across the yard towards us.

'Jinny . . . look out!' I shrieked, but I was too late. She dashed out right under the hooves of the man on the horse, he had no time to avoid her. The horse reared up, and in another second those cruel hooves would have come smashing down on that dark little head.

I froze. I was completely useless, rooted to the spot in horror. But in that heart-stopping second Blue flung himself forward. It was all over so quickly that I hardly saw what happened. He just seemed to fly across the ground, and scooped Jinny up into his arms.

The rider flung himself off the horse, and held its head, stroking it and talking soothingly. He threw a scared glance at his boss. 'I'm sorry . . . I couldn't help it . . . she just came . . . '

'I know. I know, Jim. It's all right, just take him away.'

The man led the horse away, and Blue remained with a sobbing Jinny clinging to him. 'Hush . . . hush, baby. You're all right. You're not hurt . . . hush now.'

He was stroking her hair, whispering to her, comforting. I could hear the tenderness in his voice. 'I think you should go in with Megan now, Jinny. After all, you gave her quite a scare. And . . . ' A smile crept into his voice. 'I think she's got some interesting things in those parcels.'

'But you can't see them *all* now,' I

joined in, with an attempt at a laugh. 'Some of them are secrets.'

That intrigued her. She stopped crying, and wriggled out of her father's arms. 'C'n I see some, Megan? Please?' She ran up to me, putting her little hand on mine, tugging at me.

I looked at Blue Malone, and our eyes met. He nodded at me. 'Yes, Jinny,' I said. 'Let's go inside.'

She was easily distracted, and as I showed her the material, and discussed the dresses I was going to make for her, she appeared to have forgotten the narrow escape she had just had.

But part of my mind was wondering . . . I had seen her father's face in that split second when it had seemed she would surely be trampled. His expression had been agonised. And when he had held her in his arms, soothing her, whispering to her . . . there had been love in his voice.

Blue Malone loved his child . . . there was no doubt about it. So, why did he hide that love? It was a question that kept puzzling me all that evening.

Jinny had her meal early, and I tucked her into bed. After I kissed her, I went down the stairs and found Blue in the sitting-room. I hesitated, then took the plunge. 'I think she'd like you to kiss her goodnight,' I suggested. 'It might . . . it might be a good thing, in the circumstances. She's bound to be a little upset.' She wasn't, but I didn't want to tell him that.

It was a strange look he gave me, a tortured look, as if I was asking him to do something terrible. But he went, and he must have stayed with her for quite some time, because he didn't come down again until Melody told us our meal was ready. She fed the hands at the huge table in the kitchen, but she brought ours to us in the dining-room, where Blue and I sat at opposite ends of the long table. It was a lovely table, but I ran my finger along its edge and noticed the dust. Tomorrow, I vowed. I would start on the dining-room.

Blue noticed. 'I'm sorry I haven't had a chance to thank you for all your work today,' he said as he helped me to a generous portion of Melody's home-made pie and jacket potatoes. 'You've worked wonders.' He smiled at me, and something in my middle flipped. It was amazing the difference when he smiled, it lit up his face, giving it a warmth that was as delightful as it was unexpected.

'I enjoyed it,' I said truthfully.

He put down the dish of vegetables he had just lifted. 'I'm sorry for something else, too.' His smile faded, but the expression in his eyes was still soft. 'For what I said out there . . . just before . . . '

'You weren't to know,' I said quickly.

'No. But I didn't give myself time to find out. Will you forgive me? Shall we call a truce?'

He rose, and walked the length of the table towards me, holding out his hand. I put mine in it, and we shook solemnly.

'Friends?'

'Friends,' I answered, then busied myself with my meal, because I was afraid my face would show the sudden unexplainable rush of happiness I was feeling.

4

The sewing-machine purred away, and the material inched forwards under my fingers. I released it, and pulled it from under the metal foot, using the scissors to snip it free. The last of Jinny's dresses.

I looked around the family-room with a feeling of satisfaction. What had been a rather dreary room was now cool and bright and welcoming.

I glanced across at Blue. He was sprawled out on the comfy old sofa, his long legs stretched forward, his head back on the cushions, his eyes closed. He looked bone-tired when he came home in the evenings, these days. It was lambing time. I knew something about that from the farm at home, but this was quite different — it was on such a vast scale. To make it more difficult, the weather continued to be scorching hot.

Even so, Blue found time to keep his promise, and found a pony for me to ride. Topsy, her name was, a pretty little thing with a white blaze on her forehead. Just the right size for me, and I loved her. Blue himself rode a big black called Ned. We fell into the habit of going for a ride in the evenings, when it became cool, and I found those shared rides becoming very precious to me.

It was a hard life, but a good one, and I loved every minute of it. Blue worked as hard as any of his men, but since the day I had upbraided him for his lack of concern for his daughter, he always spared a little time for Jinny.

He wasn't at ease doing it, though. I could tell that. He was gentle with her, and understanding, but all the time it was as if he was holding back, building some kind of barrier between them, a dam to hold back his real feelings. I couldn't understand him.

As I watched Blue he opened his eyes, and smiled at me.

'Finished?'

I held up the dress. 'What d'you think?'

'I think she's a lucky girl.' He closed his eyes again, and I was free to study his face, noting the way the light from the standard lamp fell across it, highlighting the rugged angle of his jaw, the sharp planes of his lean face.

Our truce had held, and the time we spent together was pleasant . . . far *too* pleasant for my peace of mind. We drifted into a relaxed intimacy, as though we had been living together here for ever. Nice though this was, I felt it was — for me — fraught with dangers. It was like skating on thin ice, exhilarating while you were doing it, but with unseen perils lurking below.

There was so much about him I did not understand, and an attraction that pulled me to him quite against my will. I still didn't know what he felt about me, whether his earlier opinions had been changed — or whether he was still suspicious of me. And I . . . well, I wasn't at all sure of my own emotions.

It had been a shock when Brian left. There had been rows of course, because I couldn't understand the way he had a chip on his shoulder, always moaning about his lot.

Nothing prepared me for the day when he announced he was leaving.

He walked out of the door, leaving me bewildered and heart-broken, and frightened, too, because then the pains had started and I knew the baby was coming early . . . far too early. It was only after that, through the long dark weeks of depression that followed, that I discovered he had taken all our money with him.

That was past now. I had recovered . . . I'd had to. Now this was my life, Peg and Jinny . . . and Blue. But it was too soon for me to know what I was feeling about Blue. It might only be because I was, after all, a woman . . . and I needed a man in my life. I only knew there was an attraction there for me, an awareness whenever Blue was near, a charge of electricity if ever we touched.

These last few days had been wonderful for me, and as I sat there, packing away the sewing-machine, I even allowed myself to dream . . .

The shrill tone of the telephone broke into my reverie. 'I'll get it, Blue,' I said. 'Don't you move.'

It was Peg. 'Did you have a good time?' I asked her.

'Too right, I did,' laughed the voice on the other end. 'Say, though, we're coming back tomorrow, so I'll be able to give you a hand . . . not much of one perhaps, but it'll give you a bit more free time. Blue told me, last time I rang, all that you'd been doing. Sounds as if you've been working your fingers to the bone.'

I laughed. 'Peg, I've loved it. But it will be nice to see you back, all the same. D'you want to speak to Blue?'

'No, that's all right. Just tell him I'm comin'. And Megan, remind him it's the show at Wagin on Saturday. Get him to take you, you deserve a bit of fun.' She rang off.

'Well?' Blue asked lazily. 'What does my sister have to say for herself?'

'She'll be here tomorrow,' I told him. I hesitated. 'She said to remind you of the show at Wagin.' I wasn't going to tell him what else she had said.

That stirred him to life, and he sat up. 'Of course! I'd forgotten, because we aren't putting anything in this year.'

'What did she mean? What kind of show is it?'

'Agricultural, you know . . . all sorts of exhibitions, farm machinery, livestock, and sideshows. It's good fun usually. Then in the evening there's a dance in the big marquée.' He smiled at me. 'I still haven't bought Jinny's present. Since Peg will be here to keep an eye on things, what say we go up there for the day. You'd enjoy the dance, too . . . do you good.'

'But . . . ' For some reason I searched for all the objections I could find. 'I haven't got a suitable dress . . . and will you have time?'

He grinned at me, a devil in his eyes. 'Stop being a wowser — and that means a killjoy. You can get a dress in Bunbury tomorrow, borrow the ute. As for time . . . well, I expect most of the hands will want to go, anyway. We'll have to make time . . . '.

★ ★ ★

The next morning he gave me my wages, and a hefty bonus besides, and when I objected that it was far too much he told me it was to buy a dress. 'Don't want you to show me up,' he said with a wicked sideways look — but I knew he was only teasing, so didn't take offence.

However, before I went into town there was one thing I had to do, give Peg's bedroom a good clean, so that it was all bright and sparkling to welcome her back, so with Jinny helping I got out the dusters and polish again. It didn't take too long, and there was plenty of time before I needed to set off to the shops.

Peg's room was pretty spartan. As I would have expected there was not much in the way of knick-knacks to dust, but there was a photograph in a silver frame on her dressing-table. A family photograph, taken years ago, I reckoned. Peg was unmistakable, even at that age, and there were her parents, looking stiff and self-conscious, and a young Blue sitting at their feet. But there was another boy, dark haired, leaning with his hand on Blue's shoulder. There was a slight resemblance, although he was so dark, against Blue's tawny looks. I wondered who it could be, a visitor perhaps, or some distant member of the family? But I couldn't allow myself the time to stand and wonder, I was eager to be away to buy my dress, an excitement that I thought I should never feel again lending wings to my heels.

'You'll be a good girl for Melody,

won't you?' I asked Jinny, as I picked up my purse. 'I won't be long.'

'Will you buy me something?'

'You'll have to wait and see.' I had already made up my mind to get her some story books, and perhaps something to draw in and colour. I held out my hand. 'Coming downstairs with me?'

As I turned to go I happened to glance out of the bedroom window, and saw someone driving a red sports car into the yard. It was a woman, long blonde hair tossed back. As she climbed out of the car I noted with appreciation the perfectly cut cream slacks, and the checked shirt open at the neck. Well open, I thought with a lift of my brows, almost to her waist! She looked the typical outdoor Australian girl, long and leggy and tall, with a good figure.

Blue came across the yard to meet her. I saw his face light up with a smile. He didn't usually look that happy. I turned to go. I didn't want to see any more.

By the time I was ready and had

settled Jinny, both Blue and the sports car and owner had gone. Only Craig remained, making a bee-line for the house. Well he was out of luck this time, I was on my way out.

'No time to talk today, Craig,' I said cheerfully. 'I'm off to Bunbury.'

'Ah . . . too bad.' He eyed me appreciatively. 'Some other time, then.'

'I expect so,' I said vaguely. 'Oh Craig, I thought we had a visitor, in a red car. Who was it?'

'Oh that!' He gave a wolf whistle. 'That was the beautiful Leonie. The boss's girlfriend.'

It hit me like a bomb. And it shouldn't have. It only confirmed what I had seen. 'I thought you said he was a woman-hater,' I said casually.

'Oh well, Leonie's different,' he replied with a twist of his lips that was almost a sneer. 'Her parents own the next spread. Do himself a bit of good, marryin' her. That is,' he went on with a chuckle, 'if he doesn't upset her again.'

'Upset her?'

'Somethin' about taking someone else to Wagin dance?'

I felt the red rise in my cheeks, and turned away from him, hurrying to get out the ute, and then I drove out of Noongarra in a cloud of dust, as though the devil were after me.

I didn't enjoy buying a new dress as much as I should have done. The bloom seemed to have gone from the day. But I took myself to task and vowed not to be so foolish. Nobody had told me Patrick Malone didn't have a girlfriend. It was just something I had assumed, from that one silly comment of Craig's.

I was pleased with the dress I finally bought. It was light and swirly, in a soft coral shade, with thin shoulder-straps and a silver belt. It was the nicest dress I had ever owned, and I resolutely thrust away the little voice inside me that wanted to know why I was spending so much on a dress for a date with a man who was already spoken for. In defiance, I treated myself to a toning lipstick. I didn't forget the books for Jinny, either.

By the time I returned to Noongarra, Peg had arrived home, and we were being regaled with stories, and photographs of the wedding. Peg didn't forget to give me full praise for the changes I had made around the house, though.

'It's a miracle!' she said fervently. 'Strewth, would you take a dekko at that! You're a treasure, Megan. That's what you are. We were lucky the day you walked in here.'

*   *   *

We set off early the next day. Peg told me I looked 'beaut', which I knew enough to realise signified approval, even if it didn't actually mean I looked anything special. Craig caught a glimpse of me, though, and whistled, which was good for my morale, though his following shouted promise to give me a whirl at the dance later was met with a scowl from Blue. Obviously he still thought I was about to corrupt his hands!

I was glad the dress was so light and cool, because the day was even hotter than ever. In fact I thought I heard thunder, but as nobody else mentioned it I thought I must be mistaken. Goodness knows, the sky seemed as cloudless as ever.

The day sped by. It was busy in town, and we explored the shops, ending up by Blue buying a huge doll for Jinny. By the time we had done that we were hungry, and I was given the experience of eating at Hungry Jack's, huge beef-burgers with so many different things inside them that I couldn't open my mouth wide enough to bite.

I squealed and leaned forward as half the contents oozed out.

'Hey,' Blue cried. 'Don't drop it all over your dress.' He whipped out his handkerchief and wiped my sticky mouth. When he touched me I stopped laughing and held my breath. His fingers stayed, touching my cheek, his eyes looking into mine. For a moment we seemed to be suspended in time, gazing into each other's eyes. Then suddenly he almost appeared to shake himself. 'I'd never forgive myself if you spoiled it. It's very pretty.'

He drew away, and we both busied ourselves with our food, an awkward restraint between us. Why had he drawn away from me so abruptly? Because of Leonie? But if things were so serious between them, why had I not heard of her before? To my knowledge he had not visited her, or even telephoned, since I had been in the house . . . did he treat all women in this off-hand manner?

The show was all he had promised, and more. There were so many people milling about, that I felt hotter than ever. But all the same, we enjoyed ourselves. However towards the end of the afternoon I began to wilt. Blue was quick to notice.

'Let's get out of this. We'll go back to

town and have a proper meal and a rest, and you could freshen up for the dance.'

I was only too glad to obey. In the ladies' room of the best hotel in town, I was able to wash, repair my make-up and run a comb through my hair. I gave a little twirl, looking at myself in the long mirror. And my reflection smiled back at me. I hardly knew myself. Was this the poor miserable creature who had taken that last desperate train ride from Sydney to seek her fortune? Well, life had certainly changed since then.

Blue had ordered a meal for us, a lovely crisp salad with chicken and ham, a variety of side dishes, and little warm crunchy rolls. And after that we had fresh fruit salad, with melon, passion fruit and kiwi fruit in it.

'I feel a little more human now,' I told him. 'Thank you, Blue.'

His eyes crinkled at the corners as he smiled at me. 'I should be thanking you, Megan. D'you know, I didn't notice what a pig-sty we were living in.

Not until you came and turned us upside-down.'

I grew a little daring. 'So . . . I'm not so much trouble?'

'Hmmm.' His look was enigmatic. 'I'm not so sure of that.'

But then he smiled at me, and my heart turned over.

I don't quite know what I had expected, but when we arrived at the marquee it was certainly different. It was on the edge of the town, almost in the bush — a huge tent, glowing with light, and the noise of the music coming from it was enough to knock you over.

Inside, it was packed. There were chairs and tables around the edges, and a raised wooden floor in the centre, on which people were already dancing.

'Grab a seat,' Blue said. 'I'll find us something cool to drink.' He disappeared towards the far end of the tent, where a bar had been set up. I guessed he would be quite a while in returning, because people kept stopping him for a chat. He seemed to know everyone.

Quite different from me. I knew nobody, and I began to feel a little lost, sitting there on my own.

'Hello there . . . all by yourself?'

I turned, grateful for a friendly voice, then saw it was Leonie. She looked beautiful, in a slinky silvery dress that left one shoulder bare . . . like a Greek goddess. She perched on the chair I was saving for Blue, and smiled at me. Her lips made a perfect curve.

'So you're the Megan I've been hearing about.' She tilted her head on one side. 'I must say they are very lucky to get you. Good hired house help is so difficult to find these days. Are you enjoying life at Noongarra?'

Swallowing resentment that felt as bitter as gall, I muttered something bright about how I loved it. I felt properly put in my place.

'That's nice,' Leonie said. She leaned forward and patted my hand. 'I'm glad Patrick brought you. He's very kind, don't you think? But if they don't treat you well, I'll always find you a job at our place.' Then she gave a tinkling laugh. 'Mind you . . . there wouldn't be much point in that, would there? It would be the same thing in the end . . . '

I frowned. 'I'm sorry? I think you've lost me.'

'Why, when Blue and I are married, of course.' Then she looked around in mock alarm, and placed a perfectly manicured finger on her lips. 'Ssh! I shouldn't have said anything. It's meant to be a secret. We're not telling anybody just yet. You won't say a word, will you?'

I assured her that I would not. Indeed I didn't feel like talking to anybody about anything. I had the sudden urge to run out into the darkness, and let the hot tears I could feel behind my eyes spill out. But I couldn't. I had to sit there, smiling at her and making small talk. It was almost a relief when Blue arrived back, carrying two glasses of cold lager.

'Darling!' Leonie leaped up and kissed his cheek. 'I've been waiting for you. You must dance with me.' She tugged at him. 'Come on, Mrs Roberts won't mind.' She looked around her. 'I'm sure lots of the hands are dying to dance with her. They won't want her boss hanging round.'

She whisked him on to the floor, and I was left disconsolately sipping my lager, and wishing I had never come. So they were to be married. Why hadn't he told me? Why hadn't he said something. I let anger bubble up inside me, it was better than the empty lost feeling that was threatening to engulf me.

'Hey, Megan, give us a dance then.'

I looked up. 'Oh hello Craig . . . I'm not sure . . . '

'Come on.' He didn't give me much chance to refuse, but taking my hand pulled me up and dragged me on to the dance-floor. The next minute I was in his arms.

He was a good dancer, I'll give him that, but it was too packed to indulge in any fancy footwork. Craig didn't mind that, though, it was just an excuse to hold me close, and I soon found myself in an ardent clasp, his cheek pressed against mine.

'Relax, sweetheart,' he breathed in my ear. 'Enjoy yourself.'

Just at that moment Blue and Leonie glided past. He was looking down into her face, smiling, and she was pressed so close to him that they might as well have been glued together. Then Blue looked up and saw me. I pretended I hadn't noticed, and snuggled up closer to Craig, laughing at something he was saying.

'That's my girl,' he breathed heavily. 'Boy, am I going to give you a good time tonight.'

Suddenly everything seemed to be pressing in on me. Craig's arms, holding me too tight; the band, playing too loudly; the people, milling about; the heat. I pushed away from Craig.

'Hey, what's the matter?' he grumbled. I realised he had already had more than enough to drink.

'Nothing, Craig, really,' I said quickly.

'It's just that . . . it's so hot in here.'

He gave a slow smile. 'You're right there, darlin'. Come on, let's get out of it. You need a breath of fresh air.'

Again, he didn't really give me a chance to say anything, but bulldozed his way through the crowds, pulling me after him. We emerged into the fresh air. It was still warm and balmy out there, but at least one could breathe.

'Here,' Craig said. 'You looked a bit crook in there, I was afraid you were goin' to pass out or something. Come over here, out of the crush.'

I must have been crazy. I don't know what made me follow him like a lamb to the slaughter. I can only think that my mind was so firmly fixed on the memory of Leonie in Blue's arms, and the bit of information she had given me about their secret engagement, that I wasn't really aware of what I was doing. Whatever it was, I suddenly found myself behind a tall clump of bushes, with nobody in sight but Craig.

'There we are,' he said in a self

satisfied tone. 'Clever girl. Now we can really enjoy ourselves.'

Then he was all over me, his mouth on mine. I could smell whisky on his breath, could taste it on his mouth. It was revolting. I struggled away from him.

'Craig! Stop it. What d'you think you're doing?'

'Huh?' He sounded surprised, then grew angry. 'Come off it, you wanted this, too. You needn't act coy now. Relax and give a little.'

Then he was kissing me again, and the more I struggled the worse it got. I tried to scream, but his mouth was clamped so brutally to mine that I couldn't. We swayed about, and then he hooked one foot behind my ankles and I crashed to the ground with him on top of me.

Then suddenly the weight was gone. He was plucked off me, as if he was nothing at all. There was a crack as a fist met his chin, and he went staggering and landed sprawling full length in the bushes, where he lay silent.

'Are you all right, Miss?'

Gentle hands lifted me up, and I found myself crying on someone's shoulder.

'You're all right. You're safe now. Here . . . use my hanky.'

Shakily I pulled my dress up to cover myself, trying to fasten the straps in some way, so that it would stay up.

'Here,' said my rescuer. 'You can't see to do that here, it's too dark. Let's walk towards the marquee.'

'Oh, no,' I shrank back. 'I don't want anyone to see me . . . '

'We won't go that close,' he said. ' . . . put my jacket on.'

He draped his jacket around me, and I clutched the edges together as he shepherded me into the light. When we got there I looked at the man by my side. He was dark . . . not as dark as Craig, but with black curly hair and dark eyes. He seemed familiar, but I was sure I hadn't seen him around Noongarra.

'I can't thank you enough,' I said shakily, as he shielded me while I tied up my shoulder straps. 'I was a fool to let Craig take me there . . . I hope you don't think . . . '

'What on earth's going on?'

Oh . . . that voice I knew so well. I closed my eyes in despair. Blue . . . he *would* turn up just at this moment. When I opened my eyes again he was in front of me, staring in amazement.

'What have you been doing? I saw you leaving with Craig.' His eyes travelled my face, taking in my dishevelled hair and bruised mouth, then his gaze dropped, and he saw my dress.

He went white. 'Why you . . . ' He turned to my rescuer with an oath, and before I could stop him, he had sprung. The two men went crashing to the ground, rolling over.

'Blue . . . please, please. It's not what you think.'

'I'll kill him . . . the . . . '

'No Blue . . . don't you see?' I pleaded. 'This gentleman has just *saved* me. It was Craig . . . '

'Craig?'

He let go of my rescuer, and they both struggled to their feet. Blue looked around suspiciously. 'Where *is* Craig, then?'

'In . . . in the bushes, knocked out.' It all became too much for me. I gave a sob. 'Would you take me home. Please, Blue.'

But he wasn't looking at me. The two men were still squaring up to each other, eyes locked, faces grim. I couldn't understand it. 'Blue,' I insisted. 'I told you. This man came to my rescue . . . '

'It's all right, Miss,' the other man said bitterly. 'He wouldn't know the truth if it upped and bit him.' He turned on his heel and swung away, walking with long loping strides. I turned to Blue.

'Aren't you going to apologise?'

He just stood there, staring after the retreating figure, as if he was made of marble.

'Oh . . . you . . . ' I had to do something, say something. I left him and ran to catch up with the man to whom I owed so much.

I caught him up, and stopped him, my hand on his arm.

'Please . . . I don't feel I've thanked you properly.'

He stopped and smiled at me. He had a nice smile, I thought, and again had a fleeting feeling of something familiar. 'I don't even know your name,' I protested.

His smile faded. 'My name is Seamus.' He flung a fierce, proud glance at Blue who was still standing staring at us, making no attempt to come after us. 'Seamus Malone.'

I stared open mouthed, and he gave a wry grin. 'Yes . . . that's right. Patrick Malone's no-good brother, as no doubt he'll tell you. Good-night.'

5

My mind was whirling with questions as I returned to Blue, but I didn't get the chance to ask them. First of all he strode away from me to give instructions to some of the hands who were just coming out of the marquee, then he took my arm and we began to walk back to the car.

'Are you all right?' His voice was brusque.

'Yes, thank you.' I found I was shaking. I still couldn't believe that Craig meant to take things so far. Just in how much danger had I been? I couldn't be too sure. A tear started to roll down my cheek. Then I realised I didn't have my evening bag.

Blue reached in his pocket. 'Here . . . you left it on the table.'

'Thank you.' I sniffed. I fished in it and took out a hanky.

He didn't say another word until we were in the car on the way home, and then, after a long silence, he exploded. 'So now you know what you get when you lead men on!'

I gasped. 'I what . . . how dare you! I did *not* lead Craig on.'

'Oh no? Then what d'you call what you were doing on the dance floor. If dancing like that wasn't leading him on, I'd like to know what was.'

'Oh . . . you!' That stung . . . partly because there was a measure of truth in it. I *had* snuggled up to Craig, but only because I was riled at the way Leonie was dancing with Blue.

'And what about you?' I retaliated furiously.

'What do you mean? What about me?'

'You and Leonie. You couldn't have been any closer if you'd been Siamese twins.'

He turned to look at me then, as if trying to read something in my expression, but I kept my head down, twiddling my handkerchief between my hands. 'Anyway,' I continued stubbornly, 'that was no excuse for behaving the way you did with your brother.'

'Are you sure,' he said coldly, 'that you've told me the truth about that little incident?'

'You can't mean it!' My voice rose with exasperation. 'I've told you . . . he just happened to come along.'

'Perhaps you'd better tell me exactly what *did* happen. Right from the beginning.'

So I told him everything, and pretty stupid it sounded, telling it like that, in cold blood. By the time I finished my words faltered away, and I sat in abject misery waiting for another caustic comment. I wasn't disappointed.

'I knew you'd be trouble,' he said.

So there we were back to square one, and all the magic of the day ruined. I didn't speak another word all the way home. He parked the car in the yard, and I got out and started to walk wearily towards the house. He caught up with me by the verandah steps.

'Are you sure you are all right?' he said softly, reaching up and brushing a strand of hair away from my face.

Strange how angry I could be with him one minute, and feel so warm and melting the next. 'Yes . . . ' I said hesitantly. 'And . . . I'm sorry Blue, that I spoiled your evening. If . . . if you'd told me about Leonie I wouldn't have let you take me. I hope she wasn't too annoyed.'

'Leonie?' He sounded genuinely puzzled. 'What about her?'

'Well, you *are* engaged, after all. She told me, about it being a secret I mean.' I tried to turn away, but he stopped me, putting his hands on my shoulders. 'If . . . if I was engaged to you,' I continued nervously, 'I wouldn't like it if you took another to a dance.'

He started to laugh then, throwing back his head. It came out of him in a great gust, as if of relief.

'I can't see it's funny,' I said stiffly.

'Can't you?' He composed himself.

'No . . . well, you don't know Leonie like I do. We've grown up together. I suppose . . . well I suppose she thinks I belong to her in some way. But I don't. Not to her. Not to any woman. Not ever again. And next time I see her I'll put her across my knee and spank her.'

'Oh . . . ' I couldn't speak. Part of me was filled with an irrational joy . . . and part was taking in what he had said about not belonging to any woman, ever again. Was he warning me off?

'And your brother, Seamus . . . ?' I asked.

His laughter was all gone. 'That's another matter altogether.'

'But I'd hate to think you'd quarrelled because of me.'

He gave a short bitter laugh. 'Don't worry, Megan. It was nothing to do with you.'

Then, to my utter amazement he pulled me close, and kissed me gently on the forehead. He said something. I thought it sounded like, 'I couldn't stand it . . . not again', but I wasn't sure, I was so dumbfounded. He shook his head, as though he himself was not sure what he was doing . . . was astounded by his own actions. Then he pushed me gently towards the house. 'Best get off to bed. Busy day tomorrow, remember.'

And that, I thought, was the end of that.

The next day was Sunday, and Jinny's birthday. She was up at the crack of dawn, or so it seemed to me. I felt tired out, reaction I supposed. I hadn't slept very well. I had tossed and turned, remembering first Craig . . . then Blue's attack on Seamus. Even more I remembered that gentle kiss, outside in the warm scented night. Had the day been wonderful, or a complete disaster? I couldn't make up my mind, but it had given me a lot to think about.

I knew now why my rescuer had seemed familiar. I remembered the photograph in Peg's bedroom. The boy with his hand on Blue's shoulder had been his brother. The family had been together happily enough when that photograph had been taken, and I couldn't help wondering what had caused such a rift.

Last night Seamus and Blue had glared at one another, hatred in their eyes . . . and I knew it had not been about me. It was yet another mystery, to add to the enigma of Patrick Malone. And there was Blue's attitude to women. And to Jinny. It was as though he was on the defensive all the time. Puzzling about it, I had lain awake most of the night.

But I didn't have time to think about it the next morning. Tired I might be, but young Jinny was full of energy and wound up to a fever pitch of excitement.

While she was having breakfast, Blue came in. I could see Jinny eyeing him hopefully, but as he pulled up a chair and poured himself a coffee the hope began to fade from her eyes. He cocked an eyebrow at her.

'What are you looking at, Miss?'

She wilted. 'Nothing, Daddy.'

'Hmmm. I suppose you're not looking for something? Something that just might be in the sideboard cupboard?'

For a moment she didn't comprehend . . . then she gave a shriek of excitement and wriggled off her chair. It didn't take her long to find the paper wrapped parcel, or to tug and tear at it until she had uncovered her doll. She took it into a corner, cradling it in her arms, making crooning noises.

'I think I'll wait a while,' I said with a laugh. 'My present will be a bit of an anti-climax after that.'

He wasn't really listening to me. He was looking at Jinny, and there was a hunger in his look. Yes, that was it. He looked like a starving man gazing at a meal that was just out of reach.

Before I had the chance to give Jinny the present I had bought her the telephone rang. Melody took it, and called Blue.

'It's Jinny's Granny.'

'I was expecting that,' he said, and went to answer it. So that would be his wife's mother . . . the Italian one, I thought. Of course she would ring on her grandchild's birthday, but it hadn't occurred to me that Francesca's people would still be in touch. Stupid of me, really, when they lived so close.

When Blue returned he ruffled Jinny's curly head. 'D'you want to see Granny and Grandpa Morelli?' he asked her. 'You're invited to a birthday tea . . . that's if Melody doesn't mind keeping the birthday cake she has made until you come back.'

Melody said, a little huffily, that it was only right and proper that Jinny should visit her grandparents on her birthday, so that was settled. It looked as though I was going to have a nice peaceful day more or less on my own. Just what I needed, I thought with determined cheerfulness, and ignored a small voice that told me the house would seem empty without Jinny and her father.

So at last I managed to give Jinny her present, and promised that she could wear her new dress that very afternoon.

Peg joined us. She hadn't forgotten Jinny either, but had brought her back a jig-saw and some books from Perth.

'Did you have a good time last night?' she asked as she poured herself a coffee. 'I've just seen Craig slinking off, muttering curses. What happened?'

Blue gave me quick glance. 'I sacked him.'

'But why?' Peg sounded surprised, but not upset. 'The Morelli's won't like it, he's family.'

Blue's eyes were steely, and he put down his cup in a manner that showed he was holding back his temper. 'He's only a distant relation of Francesca's, and he's taken advantage of that for long enough. I should have sacked him years ago.'

He got up and left us, muttering something about there being plenty to do if we were going out for the afternoon. I was left thinking uncomfortably that I was to blame. I should never have gone off into the darkness with Craig the way I did. And once there, surely I could have handled things differently. Now Craig had lost his job, and Blue had lost his best hand . . . and it was all my fault.

'Well!' Peg exclaimed. 'Something's upset him, that's for sure. Are you going to tell me?'

'Later, Peg,' I said as I moved to follow Blue. 'In a minute.'

I had to wait until I could get Blue alone. Several of the men were hanging about, and I noticed them looking at me with curiosity. My cheeks burned. What tale had Craig told? I wondered. Certainly, whatever he said would not have been to my advantage.

When I did manage to have Blue to myself I scarcely knew where to begin.

'Blue . . . ' I began. 'About Craig. I don't like to think a man has lost his job because of me . . . and he was your best man . . . and . . . '

He stopped me. 'Megan . . . maybe it was your own damn fault. But whatever

112

it was, no hand of mine is going to treat a woman like that . . .

'But strike me, girl . . . don't you realise the effect you have on men? You wander about like a little girl lost, with those big soft eyes of yours, and a body like a pocket Venus . . . and it never seems to occur to you that a man might hanker after you . . . '

'Me? Oh, you're joking!' But he wasn't, I could see that by the look on his bronzed face — half exasperated, half embarrassed. But before I could say anything he slapped his old broad-brimmed hat on his head, and sloped off, and I was left staring after him, bewildered.

Then, just as suddenly, he turned on his heel and stalked back to me. 'This afternoon,' he said abruptly. 'When I take Jinny to Grandma Morelli's . . . want to come with me?'

My heart leaped. 'Oh, why . . . yes, I'd love to,' I stammered.

He just stared at me, unsmiling, then nodded. 'Good,' he said abruptly. Then off he went again, leaving me more bewildered than ever.

What was I to make of that? What had he meant? Had he just been warning me about how I talked to his men, or did he . . . could he possibly . . . have been speaking of himself?

Something inside me leaped at the very thought, but I pulled myself together. No use getting silly notions about Patrick Malone. Of all the men in the world, I had to start feeling things about this one and it wasn't any use. I should stifle it at the very start.

All the same, it didn't stop me from dressing in my very best that afternoon, and I was feeling good when we drove off to the Morelli vineyards.

I found the drive interesting, and even Jinny bobbing up and down behind me and chattering all the way didn't detract from my pleasure in the trip. I hoped Blue thought I looked good . . . I couldn't tell from his expression. I'd put on a pale blue dress with a soft swirly skirt, and white high heeled sandals, and I'd used a little make-up.

Grandma Morelli turned out to be a roly-poly dumpling of a woman, dark hair now turned grey, pulled back in a big bun. Her husband was taller than her, but still thickset, a jovial man, and they greeted Jinny with rapturous delight.

'You'll both stay?' she enquired. 'I cook aplenty.'

'No, no.' Blue smiled down at her. 'I've got . . . some business to attend to Mamma. Megan and I will call back for Jinny later on, if that's OK by you.'

Mr Morelli clapped Blue on the shoulder. 'Is OK my boy. You do as you like.'

'How's young Luigi? Still at college?' Blue asked.

Grandma Morelli beamed. 'Is doing very well. Soon he'll come out and join us here.'

'Good,' Blue said. 'That's fine.'

I had the feeling he couldn't get out of there quick enough, in spite of their kindly reception of him. I suppose it brought back painful memories about his wife, and I thought wistfully, as I followed him back to the car, that it must be wonderful to be loved so loyally.

'What's this business you have to do?' I asked, as we drove away.

He turned and gave me a wicked smile. 'I'm afraid I told a little white lie there. I . . . didn't want to stay. A little of Grandma Morelli goes a long way.'

He didn't elaborate, and I was content to leave it like that. We drove on, through the fields of vines, so different from the sheep pastures of his own acres.

'Where are we going?'

'You'll see.'

We drove for about an hour. Blue seemed in a good mood, as if in depositing Jinny with her grandparents he had rid himself of some kind of a burden. I chided myself for having such a thought. How could a sweet child like that be a burden to anyone?

'Here we are.'

We had left the road, and were bumping and lurching along a sandy track, and I realised that without my noticing it we had been making for the sea. We came to a halt in some dunes, and I couldn't wait to jump out of the car. I sank into the soft white sand, and hurriedly pulled off my sandals.

'Ouch!' I cried, hopping about. 'This sand's hot!'

Swiftly, before my feet could burn, I raced down the beach until I was ankle deep in the waters that lapped the edge of the shore. I turned, laughing, and waited for Blue. He came, lugging a beach umbrella and two large bags.

'What d'you think?' he called. 'Like it?'

'Like it? I should say!'

I looked around me, breathing deep of the sea-fresh air. We were roughly in the centre of a beautiful bay. The sea at my back was a deep blue and still, except where the waters lapped gently around my feet, and the sand ran from under my toes and tugged me farther in. I faced the shore, as far as the eye could see, white sands stretched.

Blue had fixed up the umbrella and laid down a rug. From one of the bags he pulled an insulated box and from it he pulled a bottle and two glasses. He waved them at me, grinning, and I ran back up the beach to join him, flopping down on the rug.

'Oh Blue, this is heavenly. Where are we?'

'Geographe Bay. I thought you'd like it. Might be a bit cooler here, goodness knows the weather seems to be getting hotter by the minute. Here, have a drink. Pure Australian champagne, I'd have you know. Can't be bad.'

He poured a glass out for me, and I took it from him, our fingers touching. Again my heart did a flip and I caught my breath, looking up into his eyes.

'To you, Megan. And thanks for all the hard work you've been putting in. It's made a difference to the place. And it's made a difference to Jinny. Don't think I haven't noticed.'

'Thank you,' I murmured, and hid my face in my glass. My feelings were so confused. Was that what this was all about, just a thank-you from a grateful employer?

'I don't know about being cooler,' I protested, to hide my thoughts. 'The sun is blazing here, even in the shade of this umbrella. And the sea looks so inviting . . . oh, how I'd love to just throw myself into it.'

'Well . . . why don't you?' he drawled.

I laughed. 'You forget, you didn't tell me we were coming here. If you had, I might have been prepared.'

He shrugged, and his lips quirked up at the corners, a devil-may-care light coming into his eyes. 'You've got something on under that dress, haven't you. What's the difference? Only the same as a bikini. And you'll be dry in a few minutes afterwards.'

I looked at him doubtfully. It was true, my undies were no more revealing than many a bikini . . . it was just . . . oh, I don't know . . . it just didn't *feel* the same. Ridiculous really.

He sprang to his feet. 'Well, you can be modest if you like. Me, I'm going to have a dip.'

He dragged his shirt over his head without unbuttoning it, and unbuckled his belt. The next moment he was stepping out of his linen slacks, throwing them down beside his shirt, then he was racing down the sand to the sea. For a moment I was transfixed, watching his lithe brown body splashing into the water, his arms held high, then when he was about waist deep he made a sudden jump, and disappeared into it.

That did it. I couldn't hold back any longer. A second later and my blue dress joined his clothes, and I was running in his footprints across the hot sand. After all, I argued, with a quick glance down at my coffee coloured bra and briefs, I was perfectly respectable.

Oh, that water was delicious! Blue reared up out of it, his tawny head sleek and streaming, brown face laughing, eyes alight with mischief. He scooped up the water and splashed it at me, and I screamed and laughed, and dived to get away from him. We played, like a couple of kids. He was a different man . . . carefree, happy . . . as he should be. And I was all the happier for seeing him like that.

After a while Blue struck out in a long lazy crawl, and I followed. But, although I was a fair swimmer, I didn't have Blue's stamina, and after a while I shouted to him, and he turned his head. I gestured that I was going back, and he nodded.

I turned, and swam lazily on my back. I didn't realise I had got so far in, until I suddenly grounded in an undignified fashion, sprawled on my back like a stranded starfish.

I scrambled to an upright position, and shaded my eyes, looking for Blue. I looked far out, watching for a sleek head breaking the smooth line of the sea. But I couldn't see him.

Then, suddenly, he burst up from the water almost beside me.

'Oh . . . you gave me a fright . . . ' I began. Then my voice tailed away. His smile had faded, and he was looking at me as if he'd never seen me before.

'Megan . . . you're beautiful!'

I stood mesmerised, as he waded slowly towards me. Then he put his hands on my shoulders, and gently drew me towards him. He bent his head, and as his lips descended on mine, I reached my arms up and wound them around his neck.

The sun burned hot on my back, and the water lapped cool around my ankles, but all I was aware of was the pounding of my own blood in my veins, the feel of his firm, warm flesh under my fingers, the muscles of his arms, the long, lean length of his back.

Then I surfaced for breath, and the sky spun in a dizzy circle as he lifted me in his arms, and carried me up the beach, laying me gently on the rug. He lay beside me, the beach umbrella shading us, casting a shadow across his face.

His face was taut, serious, and I could see a pulse beating wildly in his neck. He stared down at me for what seemed to be an eternity.

'Blue . . . ' I breathed. I reached up for him, and he closed his eyes and with a moan bent his head to me again. As we kissed again, his hands stroked me, gently at first, and then I felt the passion rising in him, and I was swept away with it . . . wanting him . . . needing him . . .

Then he tore himself away from me, with a wrench, and I was left staring foolishly up at him as he knelt above me. His face was set, taut, the muscles of his neck tense. He turned his head away, as if shutting out the very sight of me.

I sat up, and put a hand out to him. 'Blue . . . ? What's wrong?'

'Nothing. Here . . . ' He picked up my dress, and tossed it to me. 'Get dressed.' He picked up his own things, and walked towards the car.

I was left staring at his back as he

went. What had gone wrong? What was the matter? What devil was riding him, then, that he pushed me away, refused to let things between us develop? Always . . . always the barrier came down, whenever it seemed his emotions might be breaking through. Me . . . or Jinny . . . he wouldn't let us near him.

I dressed. My undies were still slightly damp, but no matter. I shook the sand from my hair, picked up my shoes, and walked slowly up the beach. He was sitting in the car.

'Will you bring the umbrella and things?' I asked him, trying to keep my voice steady, trying to look as though nothing was wrong.

He avoided my eyes. 'Of course.'

While he packed the things away, I found my lipstick and smoothed some on my mouth, with a shaking hand. I wasn't sure I could cope with this. I had fallen in love with Blue Malone, but what future was there in it for me? Was I simply laying up for myself a load of misery . . . I had had enough of that.

What a fool I was!

At last he took his place in the driver's seat. He switched on the ignition, then sat for a moment, before speaking. 'I'm sorry,' he said at last. 'I shouldn't have . . . it's been such a long time . . . '

'That's quite all right,' I said brightly, and my voice sounded to my own ears as brittle as spun glass. 'No harm done. And I enjoyed the swim.' Was that all that it had been for him, a need that had built up in him since his wife died, and that had exploded in the intimacy of the occasion?

His fingers tightened on the steering-wheel, I could see his knuckles whitening. 'But you don't understand. I meant . . . oh hell . . . never mind.'

He started up the car, and we drove back to the Morelli's vineyard, with him driving in grim silence, and me taking an exaggerated interest in the scenery, all the way.

6

I was glad when we picked up Jinny, she had so much chatter that it wasn't necessary for anyone else to speak. She was clutching a big teddy-bear that her grandparents had given her, and on the pretext of looking at it, I climbed into the back of the car with her. Anything, to avoid sitting next to Blue in stony silence.

I noticed Blue taking Mr Morelli to one side, before he joined us. Perhaps he was telling him about Craig. I saw them glance towards me, and my cheeks burned. Jinny's Grandad would probably blame me. What would he have thought if he had seen me a little while since? . . . Perhaps Blue's original estimate of me was right. I was trouble.

I played in the back of the car with Jinny, until she grew tired and crept into my lap, the teddy abandoned.

Before long she was asleep, and I held her warm little body, my cheek against her soft curls.

I think I must have dozed myself, tired out with warring emotions, because the next thing I knew we were driving through the gate to Noongarra. There was a strange car in the yard. I was just waking up Jinny and had moved her off me, wondering who it belonged to, when I saw Peg coming out on to the verandah, and with her was Seamus Malone.

'What the hell!' Blue was out of the car in a flash, but I was as quick. I grabbed his arm. 'Blue . . . ' I pleaded. 'Not before Jinny, please.'

Jinny scampered ahead of us, and I saw Seamus bend down and kiss her, then give her something. Then Peg took her, and she and Jinny went indoors. Seamus came slowly down the steps. The two men faced up to each other. There was something about them that was so alike, in spite of their different colouring, and now they were both as stiff as fighting roosters.

'What are you doing here?' Blue asked in a voice as cold as the day was hot.

Seamus tilted his dark head to one side, and smiled provocatively. His black eyes sparkled dangerously. 'Sure, and can't I come to give me own niece a present.'

'You have no right . . . ' Blue ground out. 'And please cut out the phoney Irish.'

Seamus shrugged. 'I have every right . . . to my accent . . . or to see Jinny. In fact . . . ' He paused, and his lip curled in what might almost be a sneer. 'I claim less right than you would give me credit for!'

Blue lunged forward, but I clung on to him. Seamus turned towards his car, then looked back. 'There was another reason for my coming. There was an electric storm down Boyup Brook way. We spent yesterday fighting fires. There doesn't seem to be any danger of them coming this way, though . . . but I thought I'd better warn you.'

He left, and Blue shook me off and went stalking off towards the sheds. I guessed we wouldn't see much of him that evening. The incident had given me plenty to think about. Somehow, it all seemed tied up. Whatever the trouble was between Blue and his brother, that was all part of the way Blue was . . . and that affected me. Surely Peg must know, I thought. She would have to tell me, she *must*. I couldn't go on like this, not knowing what was wrong.

I left it until we had all gone to bed. I didn't want any interruptions. I tied my old robe around me, and waited until nobody was stirring, then I crept along to Peg's room, and knocked on the door.

She was a while in answering, then I heard the light click on, and saw the brightness of it shining out from under the door.

'Come in.'

She looked surprised when she saw who it was. 'Oh, it's you Megan dear. I thought it might be Jinny, not feeling too good. Melody insisted on her having some birthday cake, and I gather the Morelli's had already stuffed her like a turkey. What's the matter . . . are you not well?' She reached out for her glasses, peering at me over them. Her short hair was standing on end.

'I'm sorry to disturb you, Peg. But I just had to talk to you. I had to know . . . what is the trouble between Blue and Seamus? And why . . . why Blue is the way he is . . . you must know what I mean.'

She gave me a dubious look, but my desperation must have got through to her, and she shook her head slowly. 'Oh, my dear. I was afraid this might happen. I had hoped . . . but I didn't want you to get hurt.'

'Please, Peg.' I was very near to tears. 'If I knew, perhaps I'd understand. I can't stand this . . . '

'Hush . . . ' She patted the bed beside her. 'Sit down girl, I guess you had better know, at that.'

I sat down beside her, and she took my hand in hers. 'Francesca Morelli was a lovely girl,' she began. She looked at me directly. 'And I mean that. She wasn't just beautiful . . . she was kind, and bright, and thoughtful. Blue worshipped her.'

Peg paused, to pull up her pillows behind her, and I helped her get settled, but I knew that really she was playing for time, marshalling her thoughts.

The trouble, it seemed, had been in transplanting Francesca from the warmth of the Morelli tribe to the very different atmosphere of Noongarra.

'You see,' Peg said, 'she'd been used to a lot of family around her — you know what the Italian families are like. Lots of aunts and cousins and so on, lots of noise and chatter, and laughter.'

There hadn't been so much of that at Noongarra. The old folks had died some time since, and Blue and Seamus had to work hard.

'The sheep station was being built up, and it was doing well . . . better than ever before . . . and Blue was determined that it should be the best round abouts. He wanted it for Francesca.'

Peg looked thoughtful. 'I suppose I could have stuck around more. I admit, I like being out on horseback. Should have been a boy, really. That meant Francesca was left alone a great deal.'

She had her cousin, Craig, to chat to whenever he was around, and eventually her young brother, Luigi, came to stay . . . but he seemed to be more trouble than he was worth. 'A wild one, that,' Peg said. 'Always off to the town, getting into scrapes. Until after Francesca died, then that sobered him up, and he went off to agricultural college.'

'Didn't Blue see? That she was unhappy, I mean?' I asked. I couldn't imagine Blue not caring, not doing his best to keep his young wife happy.

Peg threw up her hands in a helpless gesture. 'Well . . . I suppose she put on an act, when he was around. She was a bit in awe of him, I think. Seamus seemed to guess, though. Whenever he was around he got her laughing. They'd flirt and giggle together like a pair of school kids . . . and Blue was glad they got on so well. At that time Seamus was often with her more than Blue.' She sighed, and leaned back wearily on the pillows. 'Perhaps I should have seen it coming — I don't know.'

'Seen what? Please, Peg . . . what happened?'

She took a deep breath. 'Seen that she was falling in love with Seamus.'

'Oh, no!' I could see it all now. Blue's bitterness, Craig's defiance. I should have realised it all along. Nothing less would have caused such a bitter rift.

Peg stirred uneasily. 'Megan, girl. I can't go on with this, sitting here in bed. It makes me uneasy, I have to be able to move around. What say we go and make ourselves a cuppa?'

It seemed strange to be in the kitchen, without Melody's usual cheerful muddle, but I made us both a coffee.

'But how did Blue find out?' I asked, once we were settled. 'Did they give themselves away, or did Seamus speak out. What did he do?'

Peg grimaced. 'Nothing. That was the awful part of it. We never suspected a thing. Francesca was moody, a bit short with us sometimes, riding off by herself other times, but Seamus never gave a hint. Not the slightest hint . . . I never knew he was such a good actor.'

'But obviously Blue did find out.'

'Oh yes. Because Francesca ran away.'

'With Seamus? But . . . '

Francesca had left one day, some time before they called in at lunchtime, as they always did unless Blue was busy in fields too far away. He found her gone. And a note. *I'm sorry*, she'd written. *I do love you, Patrick — but I can't take this any more. I'm taking the train, and going away with someone who understands me. I want a bit of fun . . .*

'Blue went mad. He found that

Seamus had gone from Noongarra, too, on the pretext of collecting some chemicals that were waiting at the station, and he soon worked out what had been happening. He went haring after them. All the vehicles were in use . . . Craig had taken the ute into town . . . so Blue galloped on Ned all the way — near killed the horse. He found her at the station.'

What had happened next seemed all confusion. As far as I could gather Blue met his wife wandering back out of the station, a suitcase in her hand. She must have been waiting for Seamus, because he then appeared around the corner, and Blue flew at him. Then Craig appeared on the scene — how he got to hear about what was happening, I don't know, but he had the presence of mind to grab Francesca and take her outside, away from it all. There was an almighty fight, until enough people arrived to pull the brothers apart. Seamus was shouting that Blue had gone mad, and demanding to know what he had done.

I stopped Peg. 'D'you mean, Seamus denied it?'

She nodded. 'That seemed to make it worse. I mean, how could he deny it, he was *there*. And to argue he'd been picking up a packet from the station yard . . . oh, that was there all right, but it was only an excuse.'

'But Francesca . . . ' I persisted. 'What did she have to say?'

'That was the strange thing,' Peg said slowly. 'She denied it, too. Oh, not that she had been running away, but that it was Seamus. But she wouldn't give any other name . . . only that it wasn't Seamus. She was trying to protect him, but of course Blue didn't believe her. Who else could it have been, there was nobody else there?'

'And what did Seamus do?'

'He left. There and then. Said he wouldn't stay where his word wasn't believed.'

I could well imagine. He had the same stubborn, stiff-backed pride as

Blue. It didn't seem in character that he should try to hide behind Francesca. If he was really like Blue, I would have imagined he would have spoken up whatever the consequences.

'So, what happened then?' I asked. 'What did Francesca do?'

'Why, she came home, of course,' Peg said with some surprise. 'What else could she do? Seamus had abandoned her, it seemed. Or, if it wasn't Seamus, then whoever the man was, he didn't come to claim her. She said that it had all been foolish, a silly mad idea of hers, and that when she got to the station she realised the enormity of what she was doing. Said she loved Blue all along, really and truly did, and she'd told this other man so. Said she was coming home to Blue, when he found her.'

But Blue wouldn't have found it easy to forgive, I thought. That was his way. He would give himself completely, but once betrayed he would not surrender his heart again so easily. Still . . . given time . . .

I said as much to Peg. Surely he must have forgiven Francesca in time, if he loved her as much as they said he did. He must have forgiven her, for in due course little Jinny was born.

Peg shook her head. 'That was it. Don't you see, my dear? That was the trouble. He might have got over it . . . even forgiven Seamus in time, because they had always been so close. But then he found Francesca was pregnant.'

I closed my eyes. Oh, poor Blue . . . and poor Francesca . . . poor girl. 'And Blue believed . . . ?'

'He didn't know what to believe. Francesca swore she had never actually been with another man, that she had only been persuaded to leave because she was lonely — and that the baby must be Blue's.'

'And Seamus?'

Peg wiped a weary hand over her eyes. 'He refused to say anything. Stood on his dignity. And Blue was as bad . . . wouldn't talk about it. I thought

138

. . . I hoped . . . well I hoped the baby would be born with Blue's colouring. That would put an end to it, I thought. But . . . ' She spread her hands in a helpless gesture. 'As you can see, Jinny's as dark as Seamus.'

'Or her mother,' I put in quickly. 'She could take after her mother, and still be Blue's.'

I didn't know why it should matter so much to me, but I felt sure Jinny was Blue Malone's child.

'When she was born, couldn't they have done tests?'

'Blue wouldn't,' Peg said shortly. 'By then, Francesca was ill. She'd done badly. I always think all the trouble and the fretting was to blame. Blue might not believe her, but he cared about her. And he didn't want her parents to know . . . not everything.' She hesitated. 'I still think Blue was afraid to have tests done. He wanted Jinny. He wanted her to be his child.'

And yet he was afraid to give her his

love, I thought with an upsurge of pity for that strong, and yet so vulnerable, man. Afraid that Jinny might not really be his child. Loving her, and yet holding back from her. As he held back from any woman. As he had held back from me.

'Will he ever change, d'you think?' I asked, hoping Peg would give me the answer I wanted to hear.

She shook her head. 'I doubt it. It's eaten into him too deep now. All the time, wondering, wondering. And going over and over it in his mind . . . Francesca . . . Seamus. He loved them both, you see — and they both let him down. He'll never let himself love again.'

She got up wearily, and stretched. 'I'm sorry, Megan. But perhaps it's best that you know.'

I gave her a hug. Then I saw her back to her room, and crept quietly back to my own bed.

Not to sleep though. That didn't come for a long time. I lay there in the darkness going over and over the story in my own mind.

Before I went to sleep I had come to the only conclusion possible. I would leave. The very next day, I would make some excuse and go. It would be hard. Hard to leave Jinny, who had taken the place of the child I had longed for, and had lost. Hard too to leave Noongarra, which had become my home. Even harder would it be to leave Blue. But what choice did I have? Staying on would only make things worse for me, and for Blue, too. Better to move on. I would make out ... somehow ... somewhere.

★　★　★

When I woke the next morning I felt stupid and headachy. A quick glance in the mirror showed me that my eyes were red and puffy from so much crying, but it wasn't only that — the atmosphere was extraordinarily heavy. I opened the window and looked out.

The sky, usually so brilliantly blue, had a peculiar leaden look . . . and everywhere was still. There wasn't a breath of wind. Even the birds were silent.

I slipped into my customary Tee-shirt and jeans.

Now I would have to see Blue, and tell him of my decision to leave. Somehow I didn't think he would try to persuade me otherwise. Peg's leg was nearly better. They could manage without me. And he would be glad to return to his shell of indifference, that I had — almost unwittingly — cracked.

I woke Jinny, and helped her dress. She, at least, was as merry and lively as usual, and I couldn't help but give her an extra hug before we went down to breakfast.

Melody was in the kitchen, on her own.

'Peg not down yet?' I asked. It was unusual — but then, I had disturbed her sleep last night. Perhaps like me she felt distinctly under the weather this morning.

'Oh yes . . . she's down,' Melody said. 'Down and gone — out with the men.'

'But . . . how could she?' I asked, amazed. 'Her leg . . . '

Melody wheezed with laughter. 'She reckoned if they could get her on horseback, she could manage . . . and they did. Luckily Mr Blue was gone before she did it, or he'd have stopped her.'

'But why so early? Why today?'

Melody's broad flat face broke into a broad white smile. 'Didn't you hear the thunder?'

I shook my head. 'No.' I must have slept heavily, once I dropped off. 'But why should that . . . ?'

'We had lightnin', the other side of the lagoon. Started a fire. Nothin' to worry 'bout, but they're going to move some of the sheep. Lucky it wasn't nearer the house. Everything's tinder dry.'

So much for my leaving that very day, I thought with exasperation. Even the weather was conspiring against me. Now that they were all out, fighting fires, or herding sheep, there was nobody I could tell. And I couldn't very well just abandon Jinny and go.

Not that I *wanted* to go . . . but when you decide to do a thing, it's best done straight away, especially if it's something you don't like. Now I would have to live through the day, bolstering up my courage to tell Peg and Blue once they returned, and no doubt they wouldn't be in the most easy-going of moods.

There was only one form of relief for the contrary mood I was in. Hard work. If I was leaving, I thought, at least I'd leave everything as nice as possible. The only room I had not really given a proper turn out was the room I was using. I'd give it a good going over, and do my packing at the same time.

'Come on, Jinny,' I ordered. 'Bring teddy. We've got work to do.'

It's always much easier not to think, if you really throw yourself into your work, and that's what I tried to do then. I took down the curtains and washed them, hanging them on the line at the back of the house. There wasn't the usual bright sun to dry them, but they'd dry quickly enough in this heat, in any case, and I would be able to iron them later. Then I cleaned down the woodwork.

After that, I emptied the drawers in the heavy dressing-table. They were still lined with old newspapers. Working like a fiend, I decided they needed freshening up, and unearthed the remains of a roll of floral wallpaper. Just the job.

'I want to play with my dolly,' Jinny wailed.

I looked at her with surprise, then I felt guilty. Poor little mite, she'd been helping me to the best of her ability for hours now. 'Well, run along then,' I said gently. 'But stay near the house.'

With Jinny out of my way, I was able to work quickly. With dogged single-mindedness I pulled the old paper out of the drawers, and replaced it with pieces cut off the fresh roll. I had reached the middle drawer when I realised that what I'd thought was a carved section above the drawer was really loose.

I probed inside the drawer, pushing my fingers upwards, and the section moved a little. Then I was able to get my fingers round it, and pulled. It slid forward. A secret drawer. It too was lined with newspaper, which showed somebody knew all about it. But when I removed the yellowed and faded newsprint, there was something else there. A flat book . . . only a small exercise book. I opened it, and saw that it was three quarters filled with small angular writing. And on the cover was printed, Francesca Malone — Diary.

7

Perhaps I shouldn't have opened it. I'm not usually given to reading other people's diaries, even if they're dead. But this was different. I needed to know, before I gave it to Blue, whether there was anything there that would hurt him even more than he had been hurt already. And if there was . . . well, I would cross that bridge when I came to it.

I curled up on my bed, and opened the book at random. The spikey writing seemed to jump off the page at me, so immediate in its impact that it was as if Francesca had just written it.

Today Craig told me that Luigi had been at it again. I've begged Luigi to stop. What would Mamma and Pappa say, and worse — what would Patrick say? Craig promised to see what he could do.

So . . . Luigi was the brother who had been such a problem. I wondered what it was he had been up to, that was so very dreadful. I turned over the next page, but there was nothing much there, only domestic trivia. But later on there was another entry that caught my eye.

Went riding with him again this morning. I suppose I shouldn't. I know he's keen on me, but it is so boring here. And I do owe him a lot.

I frowned. Had I missed something? This must be Seamus she was talking about, but it didn't sound as though she was madly in love. Rather that she felt she was in his debt. And what could she possibly have owed Seamus?

Intrigued, I back-tracked. Nothing about Seamus in the preceding pages. Only about Craig, helping with Luigi's problems, whatever they were. And Craig saying . . . wait a minute . . .

I froze. What was it Peg had said? Blue knew his wife's lover *must* be Seamus, because there was nobody else at the station. But there *had* been someone else there. There had been Craig, appearing as if by chance at the scene of the drama. Craig who had so conveniently whisked Francesca away. And Craig's looks were dark. Darker even than Seamus ... and as dark as Jinny! Could it be possible that Craig had been the other man?

What would have been more natural than that this girl, missing her own people, her family, should have turned to the one man nearby who *was* family. And given an inch, Craig was more than willing to take a mile. I shuddered. I knew that, only too well.

There was only one way to find out ... read on, and hope Francesca would become more explicit.

It was some time before I came across anything definite, but gradually the story emerged. Luigi was gambling. At any opportunity he sneaked away to the town, and although only a boy he apparently managed to find men who were far from unwilling to take him for a ride. He was heavily in debt.

She should have told Blue. Of course she should, but I could sympathise with her. From the way she spoke of her husband she sounded rather in awe of him. He worshipped her, but he placed her on a pedestal, and a pedestal can be a lonely place. If he knew of the way Luigi had been carrying on, he would banish him from Noongarra — and Francesca didn't want that. Without her young brother she would be lonelier than ever. Besides which there would be the disgrace. What would Mamma and Pappa think? So she turned to Craig. And Craig, it seemed, paid Luigi's debts.

At a price. The next entry made that clear.

What am I to do? Craig swears he loves me. He wants us to run away together. I tried to frighten him off by arguing that he'd lose his job, but it was no use. He has always wanted me. Even before I fell in love with Patrick. If I don't go with him he says, he'll tell

Patrick everything ... and Luigi's chances of going to college will be gone. What am I to do?

Reading between the lines I thought cynically that Craig probably had his eye on the main chance. In spite of the scandal he probably hoped that eventually they would be taken back into the Morelli fold, and the vineyard would be worth a pretty penny one day ... particularly if he had had Luigi under his thumb as well.

There was a gap then. Perhaps too much had been happening for Francesca to find time to write in her diary, or perhaps she just didn't have the heart for it. She must have been beside herself with shame and worry, because the next entry was in a hand even more agitated than usual, with a splotch in the ink, as though a tear had fallen, even as she wrote.

What a fool I have been! I don't know why I did it. Craig kept on at me so much, and Patrick had been out such a lot, and even Seamus hadn't been around to cheer me up. I even thought perhaps I would be happier with Craig. And Luigi would be safe. I made Luigi promise that whatever happened he would go to agricultural college, then join Pappa in the vineyard. I didn't tell him why, of course. But he did promise. Then I left Patrick a note, and I drove to the station. Oh, what a fool I was . . . and I couldn't go through with it.

I turned page after page unable to tear myself away. My heart bled for this girl, torn between her love for her husband, her love for her brother, and a homesickness that only her cousin Craig seemed able to understand. She had become so muddled that she really thought she was doing the only thing possible. If only she had told Blue!

At least, it seemed, she came to her senses at the station. She was to meet Craig there, but by the time he arrived she had changed her mind. She told him so, weeping, but adamant. She loved Patrick, she told him. She couldn't go with him, not ever. There had been a blazing row. Craig had sworn and threatened, but for once she found the strength to defy him. No matter what he did, she said, she couldn't go with him. She would run away from the whole situation . . . run away from them all.

In a temper he had flung away from her, and gone for a drink into the saloon opposite, thinking she'd panic once he left her. But just then Blue had galloped furiously up, and as fate would have it also at the same moment Seamus had arrived to collect the parcel. And all hell had let loose.

I laid the book down with a sigh, and rubbed a weary hand over my eyes. What was I doing, prying into this girl's innermost fears . . . and Blue's agony? It seemed almost indecent. I should perhaps hand the book straight over to Blue. But I was afraid to. As yet I still didn't know . . . was Jinny Blue's child? How much had Craig demanded from Francesca? How far had she given way before his unending persistence.

I glanced at the alarm clock on my bedside table. Time for Jinny's mid-morning drink, and my usual coffee break. The rest of the diary must wait.

'What time d'you think they'll be back for lunch?' I asked Melody as I took the milk from the fridge and poured it into a glass. I lifted a mug from the hooks in the dresser, and helped myself to coffee from the jug Melody had already prepared. There were biscuits in the cookie jar, and I placed two on a plate for Jinny. Somehow I had lost my appetite, I felt all churned up inside.

'Lor' they won't be back this side of sunset,' she told me. 'There's a lot of sheep to be rounded up and moved, away from them fires. I 'spect they'll bring them round the bottom end of the woods. They can't very well herd them through. So it'll take some time. It'll be safer if they're in the top pastures, if there's fires down there.'

'Oh, I see,' I said bleakly. I felt

restless. I badly needed to see Blue. It just would be today that he was going to be away for longer than usual.

'D'you hear the thunder?' Melody asked. 'Listen.'

I realised then that I had been aware of it all along. In the distance, rumbling and cracking, as if giant stones were being rolled along the heavens. And the air was very still and humid. I could feel the sweat prickling between my shoulder blades.

'Well, I hope it breaks soon.' I sighed and, taking the tray, went to look for Jinny.

She was sitting on the porch, playing with her dolls. I sat beside her, while I drank my coffee.

'D'you want me to stay with you?' I asked.

She looked at me, quite surprised. 'No, 'salright, Meggie,' she said in her old fashioned way. 'We're goin' to have a tea party.'

'That's nice. I'll go back upstairs then.'

I knew, as I returned to my bedroom that I had been avoiding reading the rest of the diary. What if I was wrong? What if Craig really had become Francesca's lover, and Jinny was his child? Would that help Blue?

It would at least clear Seamus's name, and perhaps help to heal the rift between the brothers, but would it reopen old wounds? Would it be even worse to know that it had been Craig all the time, still here, laughing behind Blue's back . . . still laughing now, even though he had been dismissed. There was nothing for it, I just had to find out.

I opened my window wider, hoping to let a little more air into the room, and placing my coffee on the bedside table, curled up on my bed, and picked up the red book again.

The next entry was dated some time later. Quite a bit later, as though Francesca had been reluctant to confide her thoughts, even to the secrecy of her diary. Certainly her situation did not seem to have improved.

I wish I was dead! Patrick won't believe me . . . and now Seamus has gone away, and I suppose he hates me, too. Even Luigi looks at me with disapproval, and yet it was his fault that all this happened. But I can't blame him. He is only young.

Oh . . . how I wish I could convince Patrick. I daren't tell him about Craig. I was going to, at the station when he flew at Seamus, but then Craig pulled me away, and he threatened what he would do if I told. He said I must suffer for refusing him. If I didn't keep my mouth shut he would tell all kinds of lies. Lies about making love to me . . . he said he'd tell Patrick all kinds of vile things we had done. Patrick would believe him . . . he said. And he'd kill Luigi, he said. And I think he would. He's crazy.

I shivered. I remembered Craig's hands on me, the night of the dance, and the way he had gone berserk. Who knows what a man like that might have done? Certainly he convinced Francesca, and she should know her cousin best. Hating herself for doing it, she let Blue continue to think that it had been Seamus she had arranged to meet at the station. And Craig went on working there, taking a delight in her misery. Having his revenge for her rejection.

Especially when it became obvious that she was expecting a child. There was only one entry, and its weariness cut me to the heart.

Oh, I shall be so glad when the baby is born. I pray to Our Lady that it will have red hair like its father, then perhaps he will believe me. For there is nothing I can say that will persuade him. Even if I told him the truth now, he would not believe me. And I am tired . . . so tired. I do hope that he will love our child, even if he cannot love me any more. I wish he was not so kind, so polite. I wish he would get angry. I do love him.

That was the end of it. I gave a loud sniff, and found that my face was wet with tears. The dead girl's words had brought her alive for me. Francesca had never really been unfaithful. Jinny was definitely Blue's child.

I jumped from the bed. At least there was one thing I could do, one thing for the memory of Blue's wife. I could prove to him now that Francesca had really loved him. That Jinny belonged only to him. Perhaps then he would be free to love again, if not me, then somebody . . . some day.

'Melody,' I cried, bursting into the kitchen. 'Would you mind looking after Jinny for a while?'

She was in the middle of baking, wiping her floury hands on her apron. 'Why, that's orright by me . . . but where're you goin'?'

'I'm going to ride to meet them,' I called over my shoulder as I left the kitchen. 'If Peg can join them with a gammy leg, so can I.'

I didn't stop to wait to hear her reply to this, but hurried to the stable, stopping only to explain to Jinny where I was off to.

Topsy was pleased to see me, she must have felt out of things when all the other horses had been taken out, leaving her behind. I stuffed the diary inside my shirt. I was going to take it to Blue.

' 'Bye, Jinny,' I shouted, as I wheeled Topsy around. 'Be a good girl for Melody. And mind you eat your lunch.'

She ran ahead of me, to open the yard gate, and waved to me as I went. I had a happy warm feeling, deep down inside me, knowing now for sure that she was Blue's child.

When we were halfway through the Windrow meadows, I pulled Topsy up, and looked around me. The land stretched away, on either side, vast plains of brittle dry grass, almost featureless except for the line of trees ahead. The sky was lowering, an electric feel in the air. No wonder everyone had been edgy lately.

The weather station at Margaret River had forecast storms. Although I hoped they were right, I found myself sending up a prayer that one wouldn't start just yet. A slight wayward breeze had sprung up, coming erratically from one direction then another, whirling the dust into little spiral whirlwinds. The faint stirring of the air was full of perfume. Even as I sat there, with Topsy stirring restlessly under me, there was a loud clap of thunder. I had decided I would cut through the woods past the lagoon, and come out on the other side.

Topsy and I had nearly reached the trees, when the rider came out of them at an angle, heading away from me. My heart leaped. Blue? I turned Topsy, and shouted . . . but then the rider looked around and I saw with dismay that it was Craig.

What was he doing here, on Noongarra land? Blue would be furious if he knew, and it would be even worse if Craig was around once Blue read Francesca's diary. Hastily I pulled on the reins, and turned Topsy around, making for the cover of the trees. I looked back, Craig was following me, coming up fast. There was no use in running, so I reined Topsy in, and stood my ground. My mouth felt dry. Knowing what I now knew, I liked Craig even less than before.

He started to shout something, but I didn't listen. I shrieked back at him. 'Go away, Craig. Go away and never come back. Blue will half kill you if he finds you.'

He stood up in his saddle, and seemed to be shaking his fist at me. 'Come back,' he was shouting. 'Come out of there, you silly little . . .'

'Clear off,' I yelled back. 'Don't you come any nearer me, Craig. I'm warning you. Blue knows. He knows about you . . . and Francesca . . .'

I didn't wait to see the effect of my words, but pushed Topsy on, though I did hear Craig's last shout of rage. 'You stupid bitch. Go to hell then . . .'

We raced into the trees, following the path Blue had shown me when I had first arrived. After a while I looked back over my shoulder, but I didn't see Craig. He must have been scared off. Thank goodness, I thought, and reined Topsy in. I wondered what Craig had been doing, riding out of the wood. Just as well the others had not seen him. Perhaps now he would keep well away from the Malone property.

I made my way along the path to the lagoon. Once there, I thought, I would veer off to the left, and cut through the bush to the other side. That was the direction that would bring me into the line that the herdsmen would be taking. It didn't take long to bring me to the point where Blue had kissed me, that first day. I stopped there, for a moment, remembering . . .

The lagoon was even drier now, than it had been then. All around me were the eerie white trunks of trees, their bark falling off them in dry ribbons. The leaves of the gum trees were as dry as paper, and rustled in the slight breeze. I could hear it. I could hear something else, too. Something in the undergrowth.

The next minute a rabbit shot out across our path. Topsy backed becoming skittish and I calmed her, patting her neck soothingly. Then another shot out, and another. And a flock of birds, bright little parakeets, swirled through just above our head. The place seemed alive with wildlife, whatever could be going on? Perhaps the storm was upsetting everything. Topsy moved sideways, nervously. The undergrowth rustled with life around us.

'It's all right old girl,' I murmured. 'You're not frightened of a few silly old rabbits, are you?'

As I turned to take the path to the left, another clap of thunder rang out. It seemed to roll on and on, all around us. I only hoped that there was no lightning. This was no place to be in an electric storm, under all these trees.

'Come on,' I urged Topsy. 'Let's get out of here.'

The path here was not so easy to

follow. The trees were low, and I often had to lie flat on Topsy's back to pass under their branches. The dense scrub encroached across our way, and Topsy picked a route delicately through it. This was going to take longer than I had expected.

I decided to keep close to the lagoon, until I reached the far side. It might be easier that way. I could always make up the lost ground once I broke out of the trees. I pressed my hand to my chest, reassured at the feel of the book against my skin. It would be worth it, to take this weight off Blue's mind.

Suddenly something burst out of the bushes, right by Topsy's hooves. I saw a quick flash of a furry body . . . a wallaby. But I couldn't stop to look, because Topsy had taken fright and lunged forward.

'Stop. Topsy . . . whoa!' But she was too scared to listen. She galloped crazily along the side of the lagoon, and I had to fling myself down on her and hang on desperately. 'Topsy . . . it's all right, girl. Stop. Stop it now.'

But I couldn't stop her, because she was terrified. All around us, coming from ahead, there seemed to be animals or birds . . . all flying or running scared . . . running . . . running. Then, of course, I realised. Fire!

'Oh no, Topsy. Come on now. Turn round. We've got to go back.' I managed to pull her round. 'Come on now,' I panted. 'Let's go back the way we came.'

We joined the crazy exodus, and as I turned I could smell it, the dreaded smell of smoke. 'All right Topsy,' I soothed. 'Easy does it. Just go steady now.'

She shook her head, pulling on the bit, but I managed to control her. We had almost returned to the point when the path branched off, when again something shot out from under our feet. I never saw what it was. Topsy reared up, and I was lifted into the air. I managed to keep my seat . . . but then she plunged forward again. In a split second I saw the branch in front of me, but there was nothing I could do to avoid it.

A sickening pain across my head, and a feeling of being wrenched to one side . . . then I was falling . . . falling . . .

8

I don't know how long I must have been unconscious. Probably not long, although it seemed to me that I had been in a weird dream world where Craig and Seamus and Francesca were performing some intricate and complicated dance — and Blue was there, too, always walking just out of my reach. I stretched out my hands, straining to touch him . . . and clutched fistfuls of dried earth.

I raised my head from a cushion of prickly leaves, staring down at the ground, brushing the dirt from my face, stupified. For a moment I couldn't think what had happened. I couldn't even remember what I was doing there . . . but then I smelled it, and my memory came flooding back with the reek, the throat-catching acrid tang of burning eucalyptus trees. I scrambled to my feet, swaying drunkenly.

'Topsy,' I called hopefully. But there was no sign of her. Surely she could not have gone far? 'Topsy. Hi, Topsy. Come back here!'

I waited, straining my ears, hoping against hope to hear the sound of her breaking through the bush. But there was nothing. Only the rustling of creatures on the move through the undergrowth, and over and above that something quite alien to the bush, an ominous crackling.

I whirled around, gasping at what I saw. Behind me, steadily advancing towards the other side of the lagoon, was a wall of flames. I could see it, between the, as yet, unburned trees, a dull glow of orange visible through a haze of smoke. I could hear it, a steady ominous roar like a giant gas boiler turned up as high as it would go.

'No . . . oh, no!' I took a stumbling step backwards, away from the advancing flames. 'Topsy!' I screamed. 'Topsy . . . help me!'

But I knew it was no use. Topsy must have fled in panic, along with all the other creatures that had been rushing in headlong flight, each one oblivious to the other fleeing bodies — kangaroos, rabbits, even goannas scuttling with single-minded purpose on their short little legs. They all had only one thing on their mind — escape. And yet for most of them it was already too late.

Even as I took my first panic-stricken steps to follow them, I knew it. Even if Topsy had still been there, it would have been desperate. I had heard enough about forest fires to know that once well underway they could travel faster than a galloping horse. And without Topsy, faster than I could run . . .

'No . . . no . . . '

Whimpering in terror, I looked wildly about me — though I don't know what help I expected to find. There was nothing I could do . . . except run and run until I fell exhausted and the leaping wall of flame overtook me. At that thought all the strength went out of my legs, and I sank to the ground hugging my arms around my body in a vain gesture of protection. And in doing that, I felt Francesca's diary still lodged next to my skin, under my shirt.

I gave a hysterical laugh, as the irony of it hit me. Now Blue would never know. I had in my possession the key to unlock him from the prison of doubts and bitter memories that had held him these last three years or more — but could not give it to him. It would burn up with me, burn to a black crisp and be blown away — indistinguishable from the other ash, all that would be left once the fire had burned itself out.

The very idea steadied me. I couldn't let it happen. I couldn't. Somehow . . . somewhere . . . there must be a way out of this.

'I must think . . . think . . . ' I gasped aloud. I had read of people surviving bush fires by burning the scrub ahead of them, moving in the wake of it before the flames behind them caught up

... so that when the flames reached that point there was nothing left to burn. But that was no good here. There wasn't time. And there wasn't enough wind to be sure which way the flames would go — even if I had the means to start another fire, which I didn't. How this one had started in the first place was mystery enough ... there had been no hint of a bush fire there this morning.

For a split second I had the vision of Craig galloping out of the wood ... a flash of realisation ... a startled question ... but there was no time to pursue the idea ...

What could I do? Oh God ... please help me! The lagoon ... that was my only hope. Was there enough water there to shield me while the flames roared across? Even if there was, could I hold my breath for long enough? I had no idea ... but I had to do something. The wall of fire was getting nearer. Only yards now from the far bank.

It took all my will power to run

towards the encroaching flames, instead of flying panic-stricken away from them. I plunged through the dry bush into the lagoon. The edges of it were rock hard, white, baked mud, crazed in a jig-saw pattern of cracks. Nearer the middle the ground became softer, until I sank up to my ankles in mud. Right into the centre I fled, and then flung myself face down into what little water remained there.

It was no use. I knew it the moment I landed full length in the lagoon, hitting the muddy bed of it with my fingers. Panting with terror, I rose to my knees, my face and hands, and all down the front of me wet and black with silt. I was whimpering now, hardly a rational thinking being any longer, but a fear-crazed creature acting instinctively, like all the other animals. I had to find somewhere . . . anywhere to hide away from that crackling, leaping inferno . . .

There it was! On the far side of the lagoon, almost at the foot of the flames, the outfall pipe. It was big enough for a person to crawl inside.

I floundered across to it, flinching away from the heat that flared in my face, reaching out to me with eager fingers. The crackling was louder now, trees were exploding as their sap bubbled and steamed. The low-lying bush on the far bank was burning. Bits of smouldering twigs came floating down, landing on me, and I beat at them as I ran, hardly feeling the stinging burns. I must get into the pipe . . . or die.

I reached it, with not a second to spare, it seemed to me. Taking hold of the top of the rim, I swung my legs inside then I scrabbled round on to my stomach, and pushed myself backwards into the dank blackness. Back, back frantically . . . as far as I could go.

It wasn't enough just to lie there though, I knew that. It would be too hot. I had to get in farther, to where the pipe was buried deep in the earth. I pushed with my hands, skinning them on the gritty bottom, working my way along, like a caterpillar. There was only just room for me to fit. Not enough to bend my knees, or get any purchase with my feet. Grimly I pushed, the mouth of the pipe receding, until it was only a small circle of light in the distance, the open door to the hell that was about to pass over it.

I gave up then, exhausted and coughing. The air was becoming foul. Was I to burn, or to suffocate? Had the fire reached the lagoon yet? Afraid to look towards the end of the pipe, I buried my head on my outstretched arms. I was so tired. So very tired. Oh Blue . . . was this to be the end?

When it was all over, would anybody think to look up this pipe for me? I doubted it. I supposed it would be another mystery . . . another tragedy for the Malone family. Though perhaps I didn't mean enough to any one of them, for it to hit very hard. Jinny might miss me. Dear little Jinny. My heart ached. She had taken the place of the baby I had lost, and now I was to lose her, too, and Blue . . . oh, Blue . . .

Then the pipe began to reverberate with a rushing roaring noise, and I closed my eyes, praying.

The fire was sweeping overhead. I could hear it, smell it . . . and I was just below it. Although I knew the pipe was my refuge, I had the irrational desire to burst out of it. But if I did, well . . . that would be the end of it.

I felt crushed, suffocated, I couldn't breathe. With a sob I twisted on to my back, my hands hammering on the surface of the pipe only inches from my face . . . 'Blue ..!' I screamed. 'Blue!'

Then the blackness closed in on me, whirling me away into blessed unconsciousness.

*   *   *

I didn't want to come back. I had travelled a long way . . . I was sure of it. A long, long way away, and it was comfortable, and I didn't want to return. I made a noise — somewhere between a sigh and a moan — and was startled at my own voice. I lifted a hand into the blackness in front of my face, and grazed my knuckles against something hard. That banished the remaining cobwebs of illusion. I knew I was still in the pipe.

But I was alive . . . the amazing truth of that thought took some seconds to filter through. Hardly daring to hope I made a great effort, twisted on to my stomach, and raised my head. The far opening seemed grey and misty, not the bright hard sunshine I had fled from. Smoke perhaps? I was surprised I could still breathe, but perhaps enough good air had been trapped in the pipe to meet my needs.

Was the fire still burning out there? I was too scared to investigate. Weakly I sank my head back on to my arms. My confused mind returned stubbornly to the question of why this wood and bushland had caught alight. It was a long way from the other fires, and although the thunder had been rumbling around somewhere overhead all morning, I had not noticed any lightning. The answer lay . . . curled in the dark recesses of my mind . . . if I could only catch it. It had come to me just before I scrambled into the pipe. What was it?

Craig! That was it. But what had Craig been doing on Malone property, after Blue had sacked him and turned him off Noongarra? Had he lit the fire, out of a crazy desire for revenge? I shuddered as I lay there. It was hard to believe he would let me ride into the wood, to what might well have been my death.

Yet, as I thought about it, I was sure that that's what had happened. He had been startled to see me, had even tried to intercept me. He had, I remembered, waved me away, and told me to clear out of it . . . but I had been too scared of him to listen.

I stretched, and tried to ease my aching limbs. How long had I been entombed? It felt like for ever. The air was pretty foul. My head felt heavy and muzzy, and my legs sticky and wet.

That was strange. I had been wet from grovelling in the lagoon, but now I felt even wetter. As if I were lying in a puddle. I eased an arm down, and groped around my knees. Water. Water? I couldn't believe it.

I felt again. Not trusting the evidence of my hands, I laid my cheek on the floor of the pipe. It was wet. What was more, it was getting wetter by the minute. Even as I lay puzzling about it, the water began trickling past me. It began to gurgle. The trickle grew to a flood. My body was a dam, holding it back. I turned on my side, and a flood swept past me. But why ..?

Rain — that's what it must be. The break in the weather we had been expecting for so long, had finally come. And when the rains came, boy did they bucket down. That was what the pipe was here for, after all . . . and if I didn't get out of it pretty quickly I might just possibly drown instead of being fried!

At least, I thought, as I dragged myself painstakingly forward on my stomach, there was a good chance that the rain would have doused the fire. Pouring down at this rate, it must surely have extinguished the flames . . . enough at any rate for me to venture out.

When I reached the mouth of the pipe I pulled myself up and cautiously poked my head out of the opening.

As I had guessed, it was over. The fire had swept through the bush and devoured all that had stood in its path.

It took all my strength to crawl out of the pipe, from which a steady stream of murky liquid was now spewing. I dragged myself up the bank, collapsing on to the blackened grass, as the rain beat down on me relentlessly. I felt under my shirt. The book was still safe, thank goodness, and I pressed it to me protectively as I gazed around in horror.

But I was alive. That was what

mattered. I was alive, and I *would* see Blue again. I tilted back my head, and laughed. The rain felt good.

I had better try to get back to the house. I tried to rise, but sank back again. It was too much effort. I simply had to sit there for a little longer, listening to the roar of the deluge, feeling it beating cold on my shoulders, running down my face, plastering my hair to my head.

'Megan . . . Megan . . . '

The shouting came from the Noongarra end of the wood. I listened again. Nearer this time. 'Meg . . . an.'

It was Blue. There were other voices, too, but it was his voice I heard, and my heart leaped at the sound of it. 'I'm here . . . ' I tried to shout, but my voice only came out in a croak. I cleared my throat, and staggered to my feet, pulling myself up by the sticky soot-filmed trunk of a scorched tree.

Then I saw them, on the other side of the lagoon, the side nearest to the house. And Blue was first, on Ned. I waved. 'I'm here,' I shouted. My voice obeyed me better this time.

Blue saw me. I knew he'd seen me, because his body seemed to snap upright, as he stood in his stirrups, galvanised into action. 'It's her,' he shouted. 'She's safe . . . I'll get her. Go tell Peg.'

I stood grinning foolishly, trying to look nonchalant . . . as if it was nothing to have narrowly escaped a roasting. But as Blue flung himself off Ned's back and came straight through the lagoon to me my legs gave out again, and I just slumped back on to the ground.

There was already a lot more water in the lake, than when I had tried to hide there, but it didn't stop Blue. He just rushed through it, his boots sending it flying up in spray. When he reached me I held up my arms to him, and all my good resolutions about making little of the ordeal, flew away. I burst into tears.

The next minute I was cradled in his arms, crushed against him, and he was rocking me like a baby. 'I thought I'd lost you,' he was saying fiercely. 'I thought I'd lost you.'

I buried my face in his shirt, and sobbed. Where was the brave little woman image I had intended adopting? Gone, now that I knew I was safe. All the horror and fear came back to me, and I was bawling like a baby, clutching to him as though I'd never let him go. He murmured comforting, half-heard things in my ear, smoothing back my bedraggled hair that was now soaking wet with the rain that continued to pour down on us.

'Are you all right?' he insisted. 'You're not hurt at all?'

I gave a great sniff, and wiped my eyes on the back of my hand. 'No . . . I'm fine . . . really.'

I looked up at him. His eyes were red-rimmed, and his face was wet. But he couldn't have been crying, too. It was just the rain.

'But how . . . ?' His grip on me tightened, as though he could not believe I was really there. 'Where were you? We saw it . . . the bush went up like a torch. How could you possibly escape?'

I pointed towards the pipe. 'I was up there.'

'The pipe? Good God . . . I'd never have thought of looking there.'

'How did you know I was here at all? Had you been back to the house?'

He shook his head. 'We were bringing the sheep round the south edge, and then I saw Topsy running free . . . and Craig's horse tethered nearby.'

'Craig!' I clung to Blue even harder. 'But I saw him riding away. Where is he? Did you find him?'

He hesitated for a moment. 'Yes,' he said quietly. 'We found him.'

'But why did he ..?' I began, then I realised. 'Oh no . . . I wailed. 'No!'

For all that Craig had done, I would not have wished such a death on him. Blue held me, until my sobs ceased.

'But why did he come back?' I finished at last. 'He must have started the fire . . . d'you realise that?'

Blue nodded. 'I guess he's paid though. You say you saw him . . . he must have gone after you.'

He hadn't intended to. Not when I had last seen him, cursing me and turning his back. But his conscience must have made him change his mind, only he left it too late. I had found safety, where he had not. Perhaps, I thought sadly, that last act of decency made up for all the trouble he had caused in the past. But of course, Blue knew nothing about that yet.

For a moment I didn't want to tell him.. Didn't want to reveal what Craig had done to the Malone family . . . not now that he was dead. But that was stupid. Blue had to know. How else could I give him back the precious gift of a child he would at last know really and truly belonged to him, and him alone. I reached inside my shirt, and pulled out the book.

It was wet, and creased up, but still intact. 'I came to give you this.'

He looked puzzled. 'It's a diary,' I explained. 'I found it, in one of the drawers in the bedroom. It must have been there for years . . . under the paper lining. Peg wouldn't be one for clearing out drawer linings . . . so it stayed there.'

He still didn't understand. 'It's Francesca's, you idiot.' I was getting cross with him. 'It explains everything. Read it! Then perhaps you'll stop this stupid feud with Seamus.'

He took it from my hand slowly turning the pages. He went pale as he saw the handwriting that must have been so familiar to him. He swallowed hard.

'And you came out with this? You were nearly killed . . . d'you know that?'

I put my hands both sides of his face. His skin was warm to the touch, the roughness of an incipient beard abrasive against my palms. I pulled his head down, and daringly kissed him hard on his mouth. 'It was important,' I said defiantly as I pulled away from him.

'Read it . . . and you'll understand.'

His eyes held mine for a long moment, then he tucked the book inside his own shirt, and held out his hands to me. 'Come on,' he said. 'Let's get you home. Can you stand?'

'Of course I can stand,' I said indignantly. But when I did the world swam sickeningly. Blue swept me off my feet and carried me. It seemed fitting, he'd had had plenty of practice, after all. He took me back to where Ned was patiently waiting, and pulled me up on to Ned's back, behind him. 'Hold on to me,' he said tersely, and we set off back to Noongarra.

The ordeal must have had more effect on me than I would have guessed. By the time we reached the house I could barely hang on to Blue's shirt, and once in the yard he jumped down and I almost fell off the horse's back into his arms.

'Peg . . . Melody . . . ' he roared, and the next minute all was confusion, and the women were clucking around while

Blue gave instructions, then I found myself up in the bedroom, rubbed dry and tucked up in bed.

It's all out of my hands now, I thought sleepily, as they left me. I could do no more. The past had been unravelled . . . what Blue made of the information was up to him. And how would it affect me? Well . . . that was another question.

* * *

I didn't see Blue until later that evening. I slept heavily, a deep sleep with thankfully no dreams of the fire or anything disturbing. At one point the Malone's family doctor arrived, a big bluff man in khaki shirt and shorts. He examined me, and gave the thumbs up sign.

'Nothing wrong with you, young lady, that a day in bed won't cure. Narrow squeak you had there.'

I smiled, agreeing with him, and snuggled down again and closed my eyes, sinking back again into welcome slumber.

Then Melody came with a meal specially prepared for me. 'You gotta eat,' she scolded. 'Mr Blue say, if you don' eat all this, he'll tan my hide for me . . . so you better!'

I let her plump the pillows up behind me. 'I feel a fraud,' I complained. 'There's nothing wrong with me.'

'No . . . but there sure 'nuff might have been.'

I shuddered. I didn't want to think about that, so I turned my attention to the meal.

I found I was hungry. Not surprising, since I hadn't eaten since breakfast, but I would have expected the trauma of the day to have taken away my appetite. Instead of which, here I was, sitting up in bed like a princess, devouring everything put before me.

It was still raining outside, I could hear it battering against the window, sliding in sheets down the glass, the sky now a leaden grey. I would never moan

189

about the rain again, I decided. It had most probably saved my life.

Peg looked in to check up on me. She sat on the end of my bed and shook her head at me. 'You sure gave us a fright,' she said, looking down at her hands, square hard workmanlike hands. 'I couldn't go with them,' she said gruffly. 'I was sure of what they'd find. And, of course, they did . . . but it wasn't you — thank God.'

When she looked up I was touched to see tears in her eyes. But it wasn't like Peg to be emotional, so she cleared her throat, and went on briskly. 'What have you done to my brother? Since we came back he's shut himself away. Reading something. Have you something to do with that?'

I nodded. 'It's Francesca's diary . . . I found it.'

'Francesca's . . . ' Her expression became troubled. 'Did you have to give it to him? Do you think that wise?'

I was beginning to wonder, my stomach uneasy with speculation. Where was he? What was he doing?

'Don't worry,' I told her stoutly. 'What's in there can't possibly do any harm. Not now.'

The only person it could have harmed was Craig, and he was past taking the consequences. I didn't tell Peg what was in the diary, though. I reckoned that was for Blue's eyes alone, until he decided to tell her himself.

But although I had so confidently told her that nothing but good could come out of the discovery of Francesca's diary, secretly I did have a few doubts. Everything would surely be put right between Blue and his brother . . . or I hoped it would.

I didn't somehow think Seamus was the sort to bear a grudge for the way Blue had treated him. And now the love that Blue felt for Jinny could be given a free rein. So the healing should begin, within the family at least.

What I was not so sure about was the way Blue would react to the knowledge that he had been so wrong about his wife. Would it rid him of his obsession, or make him worse? Would he be free to build a new life, or retreat further into feelings of guilt and remorse?

It was an aspect of the whole affair that I hadn't really thought out, I had been so concerned with proving to Blue that Jinny was his own child. Now I was beginning to wonder . . . but then, what else could I have done?

The door swung open and Jinny burst in, jumping on my bed, bouncing up and down, blessedly normal and unconcerned.

'Why're you in bed, Megan? You're a lazy bones — d'you know that? Why has Daddy locked himself in his room, reading something? He came out and gave me a big kiss, but then he went in again. I wish you'd get up, Meggy . . . there's no-one to play with, and it's raining out. I ran out in it, and d'you know what . . . Melody made me come in!'

I laughed and pulled her down beside me, where she lay giggling. 'I should think so,' I said sternly. 'You'd get all wet and dirty.'

'*You* were wet and dirty when you came home. I saw Daddy carrying you in. And Daddy was wet too. Were *you* playing out in the rain?'

What questions! 'You talk too much,' I grumbled. 'Now run along like a good girl, and let me get up. Then I'll come and play with you.'

'Promise?'

I hugged her close to me. 'Promise.'

'All right then.'

She slid off the bed and ran out, only to meet Blue on his way in. He swept her up into the air, where she squealed with enjoyment, kicking her little legs.

'Megan's getting up now,' she told him. 'She's coming to play with me.'

He slid her down into his arms, and looked at me over her shoulder, and his eyes were warm and soft. 'Is she? Well . . . you'll have to wait just a little while. Daddy wants to talk to her first. Go and ask Melody for a pumpkin scone . . . she's just made some.'

'All right.' Easily diverted, she was gone and after making an excuse, Peg went, too.

I sat up in bed, feeling suddenly breathless, clutching the sheet to me demurely.

Blue closed the door. 'Are you feeling better?'

'Yes . . . thank you. I'm fine now.'

'Are you sure you should get up? The doctor said . . . '

'Oh doctors . . . pooh!' I said rudely. I wanted to get up. I wanted to be doing something . . . while I was lying here I was thinking too much, wondering, scared to look Blue in the face in case he should see the way I felt about him.

'There's someone else to see you,' he said. He went to the bedroom door and called round it. 'You can come in now.'

Seamus strode in beaming. 'Strewth . . . you gave everyone a fright! Fancy crawling up that pipe . . . that was quick thinking.'

He hugged me spontaneously, and I

194

thought how different he was from Blue who kept his feelings under such iron control. No wonder Blue had suspected Seamus, if he had treated Francesca with the same easy affection. I glanced over his shoulder at Blue, but he was lounging in the doorway, a wry smile on his face.

'That's enough, now,' he complained. 'I want to talk to Megan . . . alone if you don't mind.'

'Sure . . . see you later,' Seamus said, then he left us, and Blue shut the door.

My heart was pounding. He sat on the bed beside me, and rumpled my hair casually. 'You've dried out now then? Anything more like a drowned rat I've never seen.'

I froze under his touch, unable to speak. Slowly his hand slid from my head, his fingers tracing the line of my face, then turning to cup my chin and tilt my face to his. He leaned forward, and his lips touched mine gently, exploring sweetly, questioning. Then he drew away. Something in me leaped, then died as he drew back again.

'How can I ever thank you?' he said. 'For that diary. I've spent all this time reading it.'

I took a deep breath. A thank-you kiss, that's all it had been.

'That's all right. I mean . . . when I found it, I couldn't help but read it . . . and I thought you ought to know. It makes a difference . . . doesn't it?'

His smile was crooked, a little bitter. 'Yes, it does. But it shouldn't have. I should have known. That's what I can't forgive myself for. But I never even thought of Craig . . . he was just part of her family . . . it never entered my head. I should have known.' He grew serious. 'Poor Francesca. The way I treated her . . . froze her out. I'll never forgive myself . . . '

'No!'

The word exploded from me. This was just what I did not want to happen. What was the use of Blue's getting rid of one obsession, only to replace it with another.

'You mustn't think like that,' I urged. 'You *have* to forgive yourself. For Francesca's sake. She forgave you.'

He gave me a tortured look. 'How d'you know?'

'She . . . she loved you,' I faltered. 'If you love someone . . . you understand.'

I knew that. Oh, how I knew it, because I loved him . . . so very much. I had expected to feel jealous of Francesca, but I wasn't any more. She had been a foolish, romantic girl. But she had loved her husband, and she had given him his child.

As if knowing my thoughts, he went on. 'The way I treated Jinny too. I couldn't bear it. Seeing her there . . . wondering if she was mine . . . or if she belonged to my brother. She was a constant reminder. So I treated her badly.'

I put my hand on his arm. 'But she still loves you.'

He nodded. 'I don't deserve it,' he said gruffly.

'And you love her,' I murmured. 'You

always have, Blue.'

He gave a sigh, it seemed to come up from his boots. 'I don't seem to know a lot about love.' He gave me a quick sideways glance, strangely awkward. 'I've messed one marriage up. A girl'd be a fool to take me on.'

What was I to do? Something there was still afraid, afraid to speak out, afraid to open itself up, afraid to be hurt. As I hesitated, he looked away again. 'Peg tells me . . . you were packing?'

'I was . . . ' I answered lightly.

His brown muscular hands were tightly clasped. I could see his knuckles whitening with the pressure. 'Must you go?'

'Do you want me to?'

He looked up at that, his blue eyes blazing. 'What the heck, girl! What d'you think? Of course I don't want you to go.'

My heart lurched, but I had to be careful. I could be hurt, too.

'Why, Blue? Because of Jinny . . . because

you feel indebted to me?'

'Are you crazy, woman?' His eyebrows had risen in disbelief. Then he collected himself. Gathering up my hands into his, he looked at me steadily. 'I'll never be able to repay you, for what you've given me. But if you had died bringing that diary to me . . . it would all have been for nothing. Don't you see that? I knew it, when I thought you were in the fire. The past is over, I've come to terms with it. But the present is you, Megan. You mean everything. I love you!'

Then suddenly I was in his arms, and his mouth was on mine, sweeping all coherent thoughts out of my head. His kiss went on and on . . . long and deep and satisfying. My arms crept around his neck. But still a little voice inside me cried out . . . be careful! At last I drew away from him, and looked him straight in the eyes.

'The last time you kissed me . . . on the beach . . . remember?'

He nodded, a smile touching his lips.

'You apologised then . . . '

'Well, I wasn't thinking straight. I'm not apologising now.' He lifted my hand and kissed the palm, all grazed and reddened. 'When I thought I'd lost you,' he said tightly, 'I near went crazy. I knew then what a fool I'd been . . . '

'It's all right . . . ' I murmured, nestling up against him.

He held me close to him.

'I love you, Megan. There, I said it! I never thought I'd say that . . . not ever again. I didn't want to. Not to any woman.'

'Not even Leonie?'

He gave a snort of laughter. 'That's different. We were practically brought up together. Leonie doesn't count.'

Hmmm! I thought wryly. I bet she didn't think that. Still, so long as Blue felt that way . . . that was all that mattered.

He played with my hair, kissing my neck. It was doing delicious things to my spine!

'That's why I didn't want you here at

first,' he went on. 'I knew you were a menace, from the moment I first clapped eyes on you.'

'And I knew, from the day that I first saw you,' I answered.

'What? That I was a menace?'

I laughed, and thumped his arm. 'No, you fool. That I loved you!'

He grew very still. 'Say it again, Megan.'

I caught my breath at the expression on his face. No man had ever looked at me like that before. 'Blue,' I whispered. 'I love you.'

For a moment he didn't move, just sat looking at me, his eyes devouring me. Then he took me in his arms again, and stretched out on the bed beside me. As our lips met, all the doubts and uncertainties were swept away.

'Daddy . . . Megan . . . '

We jumped as Jinny shot into the room, and skidded to a halt at the bed. I tried to draw away, but Blue wouldn't let me. He just waved a hand at Jinny.

'Oh, Daddy!' she exclaimed in

disgust. 'Are you tired now, too?'

I began to giggle. At last Blue let me go, and turned to face his daughter. 'I . . . er . . . yes, you could say that, sweetheart.'

She looked at us gravely, bright dark little head on one side. 'Then I am, too. Move up, Daddy.'

Blue looked into my eyes . . . a long deep look, that melted my whole being. 'Is there room for us, Megan?'

'Oh yes,' I replied, a catch in my voice. 'There'll always be plenty of room . . . for both of you.'

We shifted over, and Jinny climbed up between us. Blue put his arms around us both. I was blissfully content. All the terror of the morning had gone. In the future, if I looked back at this time, I would only remember this moment. Then he kissed the top of Jinny's head, and turned to nuzzle his face in my hair, and whispered in my ear. 'But I want you to myself . . . later!'

'Daddy . . . what did you say to Megan?' Jinny insisted.

'You're too young . . . ' Blue said, comfortably. 'I'll tell you, when you've grown-up.'

'D'you know?' Jinny said, sitting up and peering towards the window. 'The rain's stopping. I think it's been a good day.'

THE END

Other titles in the
Linford Romance Library:

THREE TALL TAMARISKS

Christine Briscomb

Joanna Baxter flies from Sydney to run her parents' small farm in the Adelaide Hills while they recover from a road accident. But after crossing swords with Riley Kemp, life is anything but uneventful. Gradually she discovers that Riley's passionate nature and quirky sense of humour are capturing her emotions, but a magical day spent with him on the coast comes to an abrupt end when the elegant Greta intervenes. Did Riley love Greta after all?

SUMMER IN HANOVER SQUARE

Charlotte Grey

The impoverished Margaret Lambart is suddenly flung into all the glitter of the Season in Regency London. Suspected by her godmother's nephew, the influential Marquis St. George, of being merely a common adventuress, she has, nevertheless, a brilliant success, and attracts the attentions of the young Duke of Oxford. However, when the Marquis discovers that Margaret is far from wanting a husband he finds he has to revise his estimate of her true worth.

CONFLICT OF HEARTS

Gillian Kaye

Somerset, at the end of World War I: Daniel Holley, unhappily married to an ailing wife and father of four grown-up children, is attracted to beautiful schoolteacher Harriet Bray, but he knows his love is hopeless. Daniel's only daughter, Amy, who dreams of becoming a milliner and is caught up in her love for young bank clerk John Tottle, looks on as the drama of Daniel and Harriet's fate and happiness gradually unfolds.

THE SOLDIER'S WOMAN

Freda M. Long

When Lieutenant Alain d'Albert was deserted by his girlfriend, a replacement was at hand in the shape of Christina Calvi, whose yearning for respectability through marriage did not quite coincide with her profession as a soldier's woman. Christina's obsessive love for Alain was not returned. The handsome hussar married an heiress and banished the soldier's woman from his life. But Christina was unswerving in the pursuit of her dream and Alain found his resistance weakening . . .

THE TENDER DECEPTION

Laura Rose

When Sophia Barton was taken from Curton Workhouse to be a scullery-maid at Perriman Court, her future looked bleak. Was it really an act of Providence that persuaded Lady Perriman to adopt her as her ward? Sophia was brought up together with the Perriman children, and before sailing with his regiment for India, George, the heir to the title, declared his love. But tragedy hit the family and Sophia found herself caught up in a web of mystery and intrigue.

CONVALESCENT HEART

Lynne Collins

They called Romily the Snow Queen, but once she had been all fire and passion, kindled into loving by a man's kiss and sure it would last a lifetime. She still believed it would, for her. It had lasted only a few months for the man who had stormed into her heart. After Greg, how could she trust any man again? So was it likely that surgeon Jake Conway could pierce the icy armour that the lovely ward sister had wrapped about her emotions?